"What kind of situation was there at my house last night?"

"There was someone skulking around your backyard," James answered. "Don't worry, I intercepted him before he made it inside."

"Is that what happened to your eye?" Erika asked. "It looks painful."

"It's not as bad as it looks."

"Did Lance arrest the guy?"

"I'm sorry. He got away."

A ripple of unease moved through her sore body. First the bridge collapsing and then someone trying to break into her house. Had she been found? Had Roger Overholt found her and Marcus?

The once familiar swell of panic rose in her throat, but she pushed it back down. *Don't overreact.*

Erika Overholt had ceased to exist ten years ago. Erika Powell had hidden her trail well.

"You okay over there?" James eyed her from the driver's seat.

"Yes," she said, pulling herself back into the present. The pain medicine the doctor had given her had kicked in. Her headache was gone and her limbs no longer felt like lead. "Thank you for watching the house last night."

"Not a problem. I just wish I'd caught him."

SHIELDING
HER SON

K.D. RICHARDS

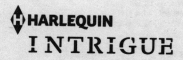
HARLEQUIN
INTRIGUE

To Justin

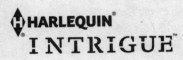

Recycling programs for this product may not exist in your area.

ISBN-13: 978-1-335-58208-9

Shielding Her Son

Copyright © 2022 by Kia Dennis

For questions and comments about the quality of this book, please contact us at CustomerService@Harlequin.com.

Harlequin Enterprises ULC
22 Adelaide St. West, 41st Floor
Toronto, Ontario M5H 4E3, Canada
www.Harlequin.com

Printed in U.S.A.

K.D. Richards is a native of the Washington, DC, area, who now lives outside Toronto with her husband and two sons. You can find her at kdrichardsbooks.com.

Books by K.D. Richards

Harlequin Intrigue

West Investigations

Pursuit of the Truth
Missing at Christmas
Christmas Data Breach
Shielding Her Son

Visit the Author Profile page at Harlequin.com.

CAST OF CHARACTERS

Erika Powell/Overholt—B and B owner hiding out from her deceased husband's family.

James West—PI sent to confirm Erika's true identity.

Marcus Powell—Erika's son.

Roger Overholt—Erika's former father-in-law and billionaire businessman.

Ronald Overholt—Erika's deceased husband.

Lance Webb—Carling Lake sheriff.

Daisy Harding—Erika's best friend.

Ellis Hanes—Rival B and B owner and businessman in Carling Lake.

Chapter One

"Just a little farther," Erika Powell encouraged, shooting a glance over her shoulder. Daisy Hargrove, the town librarian and the closest thing Erika had to a best friend, followed several paces behind Erika.

"Ugh. You said that half a mile ago. My legs are ready to give out." Daisy rubbed her back through her designer fleece, emphasizing her point.

Erika ignored her friend's complaints. Daisy had been all for adding hiking to their regular exercise routine when Erika had suggested it in April, but as summer gave way to autumn and then a new year, her enthusiasm for the great outdoors had waned.

In fairness, they'd never walked this far or this long before, but a restlessness had settled over Erika several days ago that she hadn't been able to shake. She'd hoped a nice long hike might help settle her nerves, but it hadn't worked. Marching ahead anyway, she traversed the packed dirt path that cut through the twenty-seven acre plot of land she'd purchased two years earlier.

"I thought you wanted to lose ten pounds before spring," Erika reminded her friend.

"I do," Daisy huffed. "But I didn't plan to lose them all in one day." She stopped, hunching over with her hands on her knees.

Erika did a one-eighty, marching in place so her heart rate wouldn't slow and she could see her friend. Daisy's alabaster skin was flushed pink and a bead of sweat trickled from under the wool cap she wore despite the frosty January air. She and Daisy put truth to the saying "opposites attract" in almost every way. Daisy was twenty-nine, petite with a blond bob, and eyes as blue as a cloudless sky. A stark contrast to Erika's five-foot-ten slim, muscled frame and brown skin. And those were just the physical differences. Daisy was gregarious and outgoing, but preferred to fill her down time indoors reading, a sought-after characteristic in a town librarian. Erika would much rather spend what little free time she had—after caring for her ten-year-old son, Marcus, and converting the large farmhouse they lived in into a bed-and-breakfast—exploring out among nature.

"Come on. The bluff is just up ahead, and the view is so worth it," Erika cajoled. "This is one place that's definitely going to be on the list of tours I offer my guests."

Erika couldn't stop a tiny thrill of excitement coursing through her when she thought about the B&B. Her B&B. Years of scrimping and saving, first to purchase the seven-bedroom, four-bathroom farmhouse just east of downtown Carling Lake were finally going to pay off.

Daisy started walking again. "I haven't seen Sam's guys working on the house lately. How are the renovations going?"

Erika felt her lips twist into a frown.

Daisy's brows rose. "Uh-oh. That face. What happened?"

Erika blew out a heavy sigh. As excited about the B&B as she was, the renovations were another story. "Sam's guys haven't shown up to work on the house for a few days now. And Sam hasn't been answering my calls."

Daisy waved away her hand. "Oh, well, you know contractors. Sam's pretty reliable, though. I wouldn't worry."

"All I do is worry lately. Starting the B&B is like having another child." Erika kicked a rock on the dirt path. It rolled ahead of her. "The B&B's location, on the Carling Mountain, surrounded by nature, literally steps away from the lake, is idyllic. And I'm hoping it leads some customers to choose Carling Mountain B&B over Ellis Hanes's place in town."

Daisy made a face as if she'd smelled something foul. "Is Ellis still giving you a hard time?"

"Is grass green?" Erika rolled her eyes and kicked the rock again, this time harder, sending it skittering into the tall brush along the sides of the trail. "He's been telling anyone who'll listen that my property isn't zoned for a B&B."

Daisy snorted. "Now I know that's a lie. You and I went through the town records ourselves."

To save attorney's fees, Erika had done her own research into area zoning, local business regulations, variances and licenses. The former library had been of little help. But Daisy's arrival a year ago had been a big boost to the fact-finding effort. Daisy had thrown herself into helping Erika with her research, calling the county and state authorities and facilitating interlibrary loan requests from other area libraries.

"The Dellosas ran their B&B out of your farmhouse for twenty-eight years," Daisy said with a shake of her head. "The family that bought it from them used it as a private residence, but that wouldn't change the zoning."

Erika exhaled. "I know. I even had Warren McClaine look into it and he said the same thing." Warren McClaine, like his father and grandfather, was the sole attorney with a practice in town. "I think Hanes was only trying to get a rise out of me."

"Sounds like something that weasel would do. Don't worry." Daisy patted Erika's shoulder. "Nobody listens to Ellis Hanes."

"You haven't lived in Carling Lake that long." Word of mouth was important to any business in a small town and plenty of people in Carling Lake not only listened to Ellis Hanes, they were swayed by his opinion. The Hanes family was one of the town's oldest and most distinguished families. The Carling Lake community was supportive, but there was still the small-town hierarchy to deal with. Their hotel and B&B bookended the town on either end and employed a significant number of residents. Although she'd lived in Carling Lake for ten years, to many residents, she was still a newcomer. An outsider.

Not that she minded. A bit of distance between her and her neighbors suited her just fine. She'd come to Carling Lake looking for a fresh start. A place where nobody would recognize her or ask too many questions about her past, and she'd found that. She was friendly with everyone, but only had a handful of people she'd call friends. And even they didn't really know who she was.

And she planned to keep it that way. It was the only way she knew to keep Marcus safe.

"Are we there yet?" Daisy's whine snapped Erika out of her morass. She chuckled.

Daisy was one of the handful of people Erika counted as friends. During the hours spent at the library researching zoning and hospitality regulations, she and Daisy had hit it off. Or to be more exact, Daisy had decided they were going to be friends, and Erika would soon learn there wasn't much that Daisy wanted that Daisy didn't get. If Erika were being honest with herself, she'd needed a friend. A real friend, not one of Marcus's friend's mothers, who'd engage in polite small talk while the kids had a playdate, but someone that was hers and hers alone.

She'd shared more about her life before Carling Lake with Daisy than with anyone else in the world. Not enough for Daisy to put the pieces together and figure out who she really was, but she hadn't wanted to outright lie to her only friend in town. *Obfuscate* was a better word to describe it. If Daisy noticed Erika's evasions, she never mentioned it.

"Just around this bend," Erika said, leading the way to one of her favorite spots.

She inhaled, taking in the smell of pine and wet grass, which was as invigorating as a cup of hot coffee in the morning. Birds called to each other and some distance away she heard the faint sound of a branch snapping under the footstep of an animal far larger than a bird. A black squirrel scampered across the well-worn dirt path in front of her. A crow circled overhead. The forest burst with life and, aside from being with Marcus, there was nowhere Erika would rather be.

The path curved, and a gully came into view, feet away. Whatever water had created the deep ravine had ceased to flow long before she'd purchased the property. But the rope bridge someone had strewn from one side of the gully to the other remained, for which Erika was grateful. If it hadn't been there, she may have never seen the view from the bluff on the other side. As far as she was concerned, it was as close to heaven on earth as she was likely to find.

Daisy huffed her way to Erika's side. "Okay, what is it you dragged me all the way up here to see?"

"This." Erika spread her arms wide, feeling as if she could almost wrap them around the forest.

One of Daisy's eyebrows rose in a sharp arc. "A dried-out gully?"

"No. Not the gully. The view. Come." Erika moved toward the rope bridge. "It's better on the other side."

Daisy eyed the wood slats with undisguised suspicion. "Are you sure that thing is safe?"

"Of course." Erika threw the words over her shoulder as she started across. "I come out here a couple of times a week."

The bridge swayed in answer as the wooden boards creaked under her feet.

Erika glanced back, looking to make sure Daisy was following, but a sharp cracking sound had her head snapping back around.

The walkway in front of her fell away.

Instinctively, she reached out for the rope beside her, but her hands only skimmed it before it disappeared. Her legs scissored, desperate to find solid ground. A scream tore from her throat.

And then she was falling, her slim form cutting through the air like a knife.

She felt the impact of her body meeting the gully's floor, but what she'd remember when she finally regained consciousness was the searing flash of pain that ricocheted through her skull just before the darkness descended.

Chapter Two

James West wrapped his hands around his second cup of coffee for the morning. Tucking his scarf into the collar of his fleece, he stepped onto the back porch of the small, rented cabin and drew in a deep breath. As he had the past five mornings since arriving in Carling Lake, he'd driven into town before the sun rose over the mountains and had breakfast at the diner, but he'd grown fond of lingering over a second cup of joe and watching nature greet a new day.

It was a morning routine that he thought he could get used to, even if he wasn't thrilled by the reason he was in Carling Lake. He'd known working for his family's security and private investigation firm was only a temporary career move when he'd taken the job after leaving the military. But his current assignment, essentially spying on Erika Powell, the single mom who owned the farmhouse next door to his rental, left an unpleasant taste in his mouth. That he'd felt an instant attraction to Erika the moment he'd laid eyes on her. Well, that potentially posed a different problem.

He leaned against the porch railing and watched the sun finish climbing over the mountains. A flash of something moved in the trees beyond the yard. A woman bolted out of the woods.

James recognized her as Daisy Hargrove, the town librarian and, based on the frequency of her visits to Erika's house, a friend of his neighbor. He also recognized the expression on her face. Fear.

The woman started for Erika's house but pivoted his way when she caught sight of him. James set his coffee down and hopped over the porch railing, meeting the woman in the middle of the backyard.

"Help me, please," she rasped, her breathing labored from running.

James reached out a hand, steadying her while scanning the tree line for threats. "Come on, let's get you inside." He wasn't sure what was going on, but she was frightened and, if there was a threat, they were both sitting ducks out in the open like this.

The woman gripped his arm, stopping him from leading her inside. "No. We have to help Erika. The bridge over the ravine fell while she was on it. She's hurt. I couldn't get cell service, but she's not moving. She didn't answer me when I called out to her."

James had come across the ravine and the rope bridge the woman was referring to on one of his hikes through the forest. The drop was at least six or seven feet onto packed ground below.

James stepped away from the woman and toward the trees. "Call an ambulance. You can use the landline in my cabin. Then stay here so you can direct the EMTs to the gully."

He plunged into the woods at a run.

The gully was approximately a ten-minute hike from the cabin, but at a run, he made it in less than half that time.

The posts that had anchored the bridge on either side of the ravine still stood, but there was no bridge between them.

James's gaze swept down and he sucked in a sharp breath. Erika lay sprawled on the ground below.

"Erika," he shouted, hoping for a response but not expecting one. His pulse raced. She remained deathly still and unresponsive.

James navigated down the side of the ravine as quickly as he could without tumbling down himself. Her body was angled away from him, but he didn't see any sign of her breathing.

He reached beneath her coat collar and pressed two fingers to her neck.

Relief flooded through him when he found a weak but steady beat there.

"Erika, can you hear me? Come on, open your eyes now."

Still no response.

He took stock of her potential injuries. Her light brown skin was sallow and blood matted the hair at her temple, the splatter on the rock next to her head revealing the cause.

He pulled his scarf from around his neck and pressed it to her wound. "Help is on the way."

He hoped he wasn't lying to her. An impact hard enough to draw blood and cause unconsciousness wasn't good. She needed medical attention now. His cell was in his back pocket, but he struggled to get service in the cabin, so it did not surprise him when he, like Daisy, failed to get a signal.

The end of the rope from the bridge caught his eye. He slanted toward it, careful not to touch it. Only a small part of the thick rope's edge was frayed. Most of the end was even.

As if a sharp blade of some sort had cut almost all of the way through it.

The sound of footsteps and voices drew James's attention to the top of the ravine.

"Here. She's down here," James called up the hill.

A man came into view, his bright orange skullcap marking him as an EMT.

James shifted his gaze back to Erika. "Hang in there. You're going to be alright. Help is here now."

Stepping back so the EMTs could take over, he studied the fallen bridge more closely. One end of the broken piece looked slightly frayed, but most of the fibers had smooth ends as if they had been sliced through as opposed to fraying over time.

James's senses buzzed, a feeling he'd learned not to ignore after four tours in Afghanistan. There was a chance, a good one if his gut was correct, that Erika's fall wasn't merely an accident.

He took several pictures with his phone and then hurried to help the EMTs carry the backboard Erika now rested on.

At the top of the ravine, the EMT strapped the backboard to a gurney and rushed to get back to the trail where James assumed they'd parked the ambulance. A question bothered him as he jogged behind the EMTs, anxious to get back to his place and follow them to the county hospital.

Had it just been Erika's bad fortune to be the person crossing the bridge when it gave out or had someone rigged it intending for her to fall?

Chapter Three

Erika's eyelids felt like lead, but she forced them open to find harsh fluorescent overhead lighting beating down on her. She pressed them closed and groaned again.

A rustling sound came from her right, and Daisy's gardenia-scented perfume wafted under her nose. "Erika? You're in the hospital. You're going to be alright but you took a nasty fall."

The memory of walking onto the bridge and the feeling of abject panic when she no longer felt the wooden slats beneath her feet came rushing back. The monitor next to her bed beeped faster.

"Everything is going to be okay." Sheriff Lance Webb's voice prompted Erika to open her eyes again.

A nurse pushed through the room door. "Ah, you're awake. Dr. Blackwell will be glad to hear it." The nurse pulled the blood pressure cuff from the hook on the wall and wrapped it around Erika's arm. "How's your head?" The nurse tapped Erika's stats into the tablet she'd entered the room with.

"Like the Penn State marching band is on the field."

The nurse chuckled and tucked her tablet back under her arm. "How about I get you some ibuprofen for that?"

"Yes, please. Thank you."

Erika turned back to Daisy and Lance once the nurse left. "How long have I been unconscious?"

"You regained consciousness not long after they got you to the hospital," Lance answered. At six foot three, trim, well-muscled with a roguish smile, the town sheriff cut an impressive figure that had earned him a spot as one of the town's most eligible bachelors. Lance's famous grin was nowhere to be seen at the moment, though. "The doctor gave you a sedative, so you'd rest. You've been out for a few hours."

"A few hours?" Panic sparked in her chest. "What time is it? I have to meet Marcus when school lets out."

"Don't worry about that, honey," Daisy said, covering Erika's hand with her own.

"Clarke has already agreed to get Marcus from school this afternoon when he picks up Devin," Lance said. "Marcus and Devin can have a sleepover tonight and Bridges will drop them both off at school tomorrow."

Deputy Clarke Bridges and his husband, Steve Sanchez, were parents to Marcus's best friend Devin and often helped her out with Marcus—picking up, dropping off or babysitting when needed.

"The school won't let you take Marcus unless I

give them permission." Erika angled her body to reach for the phone on the bedside table. A sharp pain slammed through her head and she fell back against the pillows.

"Don't move," Lance barked out. "I called the school and explained what happened. It wasn't a problem. The doctor wants to observe you overnight."

She may have spent more time with Daisy over the last year, but Lance held the mantle of being the first friend she'd made after moving to Carling Lake.

Lance had been a deputy then and somewhat new to Carling Lake himself. His recent election as Carling Lake's first Black sheriff hadn't pleased everyone in town. There'd been a spike of vandalism and a rumored illegal gambling ring had led to some rumblings about his stewardship. She knew Lance was under a great deal of stress at the moment and regretted adding to his burden.

"I don't want to stay in the hospital overnight. Marcus will worry." It had been just the two of them for all of Marcus's life. Even though he was only ten, he was fiercely protective of her, and she of him.

Daisy reached for her hand and squeezed. "Marcus is fine. You can call him later."

"The doctors don't think you have a concussion, but you took a nasty fall. You should rest. And not worry." The voice was deep, gravelly and unfamiliar.

Erika shifted her gaze to the other side of the room where the comment had come from. Her new neighbor leaned against the windowsill. She had no idea why he was there. "I…ah, I mean, Mr.…."

The nurse chose that moment to return, which gave Erika a moment to regain her composure and study the man up close while she downed her pain pill. Not for the first time this week, she noted how incredibly good-looking her new neighbor was.

Where Lance radiated calm, competent authority, James West was breathtakingly imposing. Tall, broad-shouldered, with a neatly trimmed beard and a shaved head revealing smooth dark brown skin, the man exuded a rugged attractiveness. She'd seen him jogging through town in workout shorts and a tee a couple of times in the week since he'd arrived and knew that his clothing hid a well-toned body.

The nurse retreated from the room again.

Daisy shot a bright smile at the man on the other side of the bed and picked up the conversation where they'd left off. "I had to go back to your house to call for an ambulance. James saw me and ran to help you while I called."

So it was James already. Apparently, Daisy had wasted no time getting friendly with the new guy. Erika flushed with guilt the moment the thought floated through her mind. Daisy was her friend and Erika wasn't looking for a relationship, certainly not with a man just passing through town. No matter how chivalrous or handsome he was.

"All I did was stay with you until the EMTs got there," James said, straightening and moving closer to the bed.

It wasn't nothing, especially since she'd been less than welcoming once she found out that he hadn't rented the cabin for a few days like most tourists. James West would be her neighbor for at least a month. She didn't know why that put her on edge. It was really no concern of hers who stayed in the cabin. Yet, the moment she'd seen him arrive in his shiny black SUV, her defenses had gone up. Unjustifiably, it appeared.

"Thank you for coming to my aid, Mr. West."

"Please call me James. And no thanks are necessary. I'm just happy I was around to help."

"Erika, if you're up to it, I'd like to ask you a few questions," Lance said, taking a small notebook out of the interior pocket of his black jacket.

"I'm up for it." She gave a slight nod and was grateful when it didn't set off another jackhammer in her head.

"How often do you go to the bluff?" Lance held a pen over the notebook at the ready.

"Once, maybe twice a week. The walk is good exercise, and the view of the mountains is the best in Carling Lake. It helps me think. Plan."

She usually went to the bluff by herself, but she was shaken by the thought that Daisy, or someone else, could have stepped onto that bridge and been hurt. Or, God forbid, Marcus might have wandered out there by himself.

"Okay, and I assume you didn't notice any damage to the bridge on your prior visits," Lance continued his questioning, keeping her thoughts from spiraling toward the worst-case scenarios.

"No. I look regularly. Marcus isn't allowed to go that far from the house without me, but it's not unusual to find a tourist who has ventured off the public hiking trail even though I've posted private-property signs."

"Before today, when was the last time you made an inspection?"

She bit her bottom lip, thinking. "I walked to the bluff Friday afternoon before picking Marcus up from school."

She'd gone to the bluff to cool off after running into Ellis. The rival B&B owner had intercepted her as she was coming out of the hardware store and suggested she'd regret it if she persisted in attempting to open her B&B. Ten years ago, she'd promised herself that she'd never again allow herself to be bullied by anyone, and their exchange had ended with harsh words, something that was becoming quite a regular occurrence on the rare occasion they spoke to each other at all.

Lance glanced up from taking notes. "Friday, four days ago—" his eyes narrowed "—and you didn't notice any damage then."

Had she looked for damage then? The walk to the bluff was her attempt to settle and regroup before she had to collect Marcus and go into Mom mode.

She tried to remember whether she'd looked at the cables and anchors? She couldn't recall. "To be honest, I'm not sure I looked. I was there because I was upset."

Lance's brow knitted together. "Upset? Why?"

Erika rolled her eyes. "Ellis Hanes felt the need to tell me, yet again, why I should give up on the B&B now before I lose my shirt. And I told him, yet again, where he could stick his faux concern. We made a bit of a scene in front of Laureano's hardware."

James's mouth twitched, a sexy almost-smile turning his lips up and adding a twinkle to his eye.

Whoa. She must have hit her head harder than the doctors thought.

"How am I just now hearing about this?" Lance asked with a chuckle, bringing her back to the conversation.

Erika shifted her gaze from James's face to Lance's. "Because you've been busy dealing with the vandalism cases and that underground gambling ring that's got everyone in town talking."

"And making eyes at that new waitress at Mahoney's Grill," Daisy interjected.

Lance shot Daisy a quelling look. Daisy winked.

"Excuse me," James's deep voice rumbled through the room. "Being new to town, I'm not familiar with names. Who is Ellis Hanes?"

"A giant tool, and Erika's nemesis," Daisy spat.

Erika slapped her friend's hand lightly. "He's not my nemesis." She looked at James. "Ellis owns the Carling Lake Hotel and the Carling Lake B&B. He's not happy I'm set to become the competition."

"Even though the town gets more than enough

tourism to support an additional B&B." Daisy frowned. "As it is, during the tourist season, all the hotels within a fifteen-mile radius are booked solid."

"Yes, but that allows Ellis to jack up the prices of his rooms to ridiculous levels," Lance said.

"I see." James massaged the dark stubble covering his square jaw. He focused on a spot on the wall and a groove cut a line through his forehead as if he were thinking deeply.

Lance cleared his throat. "Getting back to my question. You can't say for sure there was no damage to the bridge last Friday?"

"Not for sure," Erika said. Lance shot a glance across the room at James. She looked from one man to the other. "What was that look?"

"Nothing for you to worry about." Lance closed his notebook and slid it back into the inner pocket of his coat. "I should have a preliminary report for your insurance company by next week."

Her insurance premium was already set to increase significantly when the B&B officially opened. Reporting the bridge's collapse meant her premium would skyrocket. An expense she neither needed nor could afford. Still, she wasn't going to let Lance blow her off.

"Are you thinking my fall wasn't an accident?" She pushed herself up straighter in the bed.

"I don't want you to worry. My office is going to investigate." Lance shot another conspicuous look at James. But her neighbor's eyes were locked in on her face.

"I told the sheriff that the rope looked like it had been cut. At least partially," James said.

Lance hissed a swear and pinned James with a glare.

James held the sheriff's gaze. "She has a right to know."

Erika couldn't focus on the disagreement between the men. The room had shrunk rapidly until it felt as if there wasn't enough air left in the room to inhale a breath. A voice she hadn't heard in years whispered through her mind.

If you ever try to leave me, I'll find you and I'll kill you.

It had been a long time since she'd thought of the man who'd regularly uttered those words.

But even if the bridge had been tampered with, Ronald couldn't have done it.

Ronald was dead. She was sure of that.

"Erika, you okay?" Daisy asked, pulling the men's attention from each other and focusing it on her.

"I'm fine," Erika said, looking from Daisy to Lance. "Really, Lance, I'm okay. The idea that this might have been something other than an accident threw me for a minute, that's all."

"We don't know it wasn't an accident," Lance snapped. "That snowstorm last week had extremely high winds. It's possible something clipped the bridge. As I said, we'll know more once we investigate."

James's brow arched into a dubious expression.

Erika offered a wan smile.

"You're probably right. That storm was massive. And I promise I won't worry until I know there's something to worry about." It was a lie, but one of many she'd told her friends since they'd met.

"I need to get going." Lance moved toward the door. "Can I give you a lift, Daisy?"

"No. I'm going to stay the night here with Erika," Daisy said, pulling her chair closer to the bed.

"Daisy, no. There's no reason for you to spend the night in an uncomfortable chair."

"I want to. I don't want you to be alone in the hospital."

Erika waved her off. "I can't ask you to do that. Not when I need another favor from you. Do you think you can pick me up tomorrow morning when I'm discharged?"

Daisy's nose crinkled. "Oh, I'm scheduled to open the library tomorrow, but I'm sure I can get someone to cover my shift." But the tone of her voice contradicted her words.

Like most local government agencies, there was never enough money in the library's coffers, and Daisy had complained more than once that she did the work of three full-time librarians.

Erika felt a stab of guilt for adding to her friend's load. "Don't worry about it. I can call a cab."

Daisy's bob shook. "No way—"

"I can give you a ride," James cut Daisy off.

Erika didn't hide her surprise. "I can't ask you to do that."

"Really, it's not a problem." James smiled, revealing a dimple in each cheek and confirming her earlier thoughts.

Definitely sexy.

"I come into town every morning for breakfast. I can swing by after and pick you up."

There was no reason to decline, except that she didn't like relying on others. Especially strangers. But he was her neighbor, and he had rushed to her aid. And it was only a ride.

"If it's not too much trouble."

"No trouble at all," James said.

Daisy, then Lance, gave her a gingerly hug before heading for the hospital room door.

James followed them, turning back before crossing into the hall. "I'll be here by nine."

At the answering nod, he let the door snap shut softly behind him.

Erika reclined on the uncomfortable hospital pillows. Her headache was slowly receding, making clear-headed thought possible. She'd moved to Carling Lake when Marcus was still a baby. It had taken years for her to feel safe, to trust, but she'd gotten there. Now an old familiar fear lurked.

Had her past finally come back to haunt her?

Chapter Four

Sketching usually helped James clear his head and relax, but tonight his mind wouldn't slow down. He laid the charcoal pencil next to his half-finished drawing and rolled his shoulders. The sketch he'd been working on for the last several days, a farmhouse perched on a slight incline overlooking a vast lake, had called out to him from the moment he'd seen it. The sketch was a far cry from the gritty cityscapes he usually drew. The hip avant-garde New York gallery that had recently sold two of his pieces and had been gently pressuring him for more would probably laugh in his face if he presented them with this piece. But then he already knew he'd never sell this sketch. Gift it, maybe.

James's gaze wandered to the window. Erika's farmhouse was dark and serene. He'd checked that all the doors were locked, and the windows secured when he'd returned from the hospital. But he couldn't shake the feeling that there was more to Erika's fall than a simple accident.

His phone rang, pulling him from his musings. He said, heading for the kitchen.

"How's it going?" Ryan asked without preamble.

"I'm working on it," James answered evenly, grabbing a beer from the fridge.

Although he was six years James's junior, Ryan helmed West Security and Investigations, the security firm that their father had started two decades ago. That made his younger brother his boss, at least for the time being.

"You've been there for five days already. Are you making any progress?" Ryan asked impatiently.

"I'm handling it," James snapped. He took a long gulp from the bottle and reminded himself Ryan idled on impatient.

If Ryan had noticed the irritation in James's tone, he ignored it. "Handle it faster. We've got other cases."

Several weeks ago, West had been hired by the executors of Roger Overholt's estate to find his estranged daughter-in-law, Erika Overholt, a task that was usually straightforward. In this case, it had taken weeks to track down the woman they were pretty sure was Erika Overholt, although she now went by the name Erika Powell. Roger had decreed that all his heirs must be notified about the terms of the will simultaneously. Erika Overholt's disappearing act left billions in limbo.

"When you assigned me this case, you said you thought I was the best man for it. I do things my way, in my time." James set his glass on the counter and looked out the window of the sink at the expanse of his and Erika's lawns heading back toward the forest. The moon was high and round, casting shadows over both backyards.

"You are the best man for the job. You love nature. Fresh air. Hiking. All that outdoorsy stuff. You fit right in."

"Right. So let me fit in. You know I can't simply walk up to Erika Powell and ask if she's really Erika Overholt. And before you say it, I will not break into the woman's house."

Breaking and entering was more their other brother, Shawn's style. He was so good at it; most people never even knew he'd been inside their homes.

But it wasn't James's style. He didn't want to break the law or invade Erika's privacy unless there was no other choice. The trouble was he hadn't worked out how to get the information he needed. But he wasn't about to share that with Ryan.

A shadow at the tree line behind Erika's house caught his attention. James leaned forward, not sure what he was looking at, although his gut reaction said that it wasn't anything good.

"James? Are you still there?" Ryan asked.

"No," he said, ending the call.

It was lucky that he hadn't turned on the overhead lights when he'd moved into the kitchen. He stood in the darkness, watching for movement, or changes in the depth or composition of the shadows. Several minutes passed, but he was used to waiting.

Finally, the shadow moved. A man. In dark clothing. The man slid between the oak trees bordering the property. From where James stood, it was clear Erika's house was the man's target.

But what exactly was he planning to do?

It was possible word had gotten out that the house was empty and an easy target for a burglar. But something told him this man's intent wasn't burglary.

James slipped out the front door of the cabin and rounded the side of the house. Whoever was in the woods was good, keeping to the shadows. But James was better.

It seemed like hours, but the man finally stepped out of the trees. He moved fast now that he was out in the open backyard. He bounded for the house like a heat-seeking missile.

James moved just as fast, tackling the intruder in the middle of the yard. They hit the frozen ground hard and rolled. Something shiny flew out of the intruder's hand and sailed across the lawn.

James noted the man's pale skin and dirty blond hair before he aimed a blow at his face. The man recovered quickly, rearing up and nearly flipping James. Off balance, James took a punch to his side and another to his nose. Even with a gloved hand, there was plenty of power behind the punches.

Blood spurted from James's nose and his ears rang. He'd had his nose broken once before and was pretty sure the damage had fallen short of a break, but that knowledge did nothing to temper the pain at the moment. Taking advantage of James's shift in focus, the man lurched to his feet and fled back toward the trees.

James pressed his sleeve to his nose and took off after the man. Ignoring the branches whipping him in the face, he followed the sound of footsteps and labored breathing a short way into the woods. The thud of heavy footsteps grew fainter as the man increased the distance between them. He obviously knew where he was going, a claim James couldn't make.

James slowed. He didn't know the woods well enough to go tramping through them in the dark. Instead, he headed back to his cabin, going over the attack.

It was too much of a stretch to believe the attempted break-in was completely separate from Erika's fall.

He'd staunched his bloody nose by the time Lance Webb and another deputy arrived. He switched on the outside lights and met them on the front porch.

"Mr. West, this is Deputy Clarke Bridges." Webb gestured to the short stout man next to him. "You called in a B&E?"

"Attempted. And not here. I caught a man trying to break into Erika's farmhouse. We tussled in the backyard there but he got by me."

Webb cocked his head, openly assessing the injuries to James's face.

He'd cleaned up as much as he could. His nose wasn't broken, but he'd be breathing out of one nostril for a day or two and the swelling wasn't pretty.

"I hope you gave as good as you got." Bridges smirked.

An open question, as far as James could tell.

"I chased the guy into the trees there but didn't get very far. Figured it wasn't the wisest course of action to go chasing through the woods after dark."

"Can't argue with you there," Webb said. "I want to take a look at the scene and then I'll be back to take your statement."

Webb and Bridges descended the porch stairs and headed for Erika's house.

James retreated into the cabin, started a pot of coffee and watched the lawmen work through his kitchen window. The beams of their flashlights cut wide swaths of light through the darkness as the men searched for evidence.

After returning from the hospital last night, he'd run a background check on Sheriff Lance Webb. The thirty-nine-year-old had served on the Atlanta police force for nine years, earning his detective shield. He'd racked up several commendations, so James didn't doubt the man was competent. And he seemed to care for Erika, enough so that James wondered whether the two had something going other than friendship.

Not that it was any of his concern, he thought, rubbing at the prickling jealousy rising in his chest.

Webb turned, his eyes locking on James through the window. Webb started for the cabin and James let him in through the back door.

"Have a seat." James motioned to the kitchen

table. He'd packed away his drawing materials while he waited for the sheriff to arrive, so the walnut wood was now bare. "I'll get us some coffee, then you can ask your questions."

"I'd appreciate that." Webb pulled the wool hat from his head and tucked it into his coat pocket. "It's colder than a mother-in-law's kiss out there."

"I wouldn't know about that. Never married." James poured two mugs of coffee and carried them to the table.

Webb took the cup with a tired smile of thanks. "It's just something to say. My former mother-in-law is one of the loveliest ladies I know. I'm just sorry she didn't rub off on her daughter."

James eyed the sheriff over the rim of his coffee mug.

As if realizing he'd plunged into territory he didn't want to tread, Webb straightened, set his mug aside and pulled a notebook from his coat pocket. "Okay, let's start from the beginning."

James took the sheriff through the events of the evening, from when he first noticed a figure in the shadows to their fight in Erika's yard and the intruder's escape into the woods. He left out that he'd been sketching before spotting the intruder.

Although he'd recently sold a couple of pieces, he generally kept his hobby to himself. A part of him, he could admit, remained insecure about his talent despite the sales. More than just insecurity. His drawings reflected how he felt about and saw the world.

He'd brought three of his finished pieces with

him and they hung on the walls of the cabin now. The only indication that they were his work was the tiny signature in the bottom left corner.

"So you see this guy skulking around and you thought the best course of action was to confront him rather than call the sheriff's office?" Webb asked, his expression pinched.

"Yes." James smiled, raising his mug to his lips.

"And how did that work out for you?" Webb said, motioning to James's face.

Point taken. He had a bloody nose, and he'd let the intruder get away. But if he'd waited for the sheriff, the man would have made it inside Erika's house. It was empty, but he still could have done damage. And there was no guarantee Webb would have arrived in time to catch the man, even if James had called before approaching him.

"We found a can of kerosene in Erika's yard," Lance said.

James felt his brow furrow. "That must have been what fell out of the guy's hand when I tackled him." Which also confirmed he'd done the right thing confronting the guy before calling for help. Erika's home could have been engulfed by the time Webb and the fire department arrived.

"We'll run it for prints, but I'm not holding out hope. It's twelve degrees out there and I'm assuming the guy had on gloves." Sheriff Webb's eyebrows went up in question.

James nodded.

Webb scratched a note on his pad, then looked across the table again. "I checked you out."

James let the corner of his mouth quirk up. "Did you like what you found?"

"You're cocky, but I guess you have a right to be. You've got an impressive military record."

James took another sip of his coffee. The impressive military career had come at a cost—it always did. But experience had taught him it wasn't a cost society wanted to think about or face, so he said nothing.

"What I want to know is what brings you to Carling Lake?" Webb asked.

So the sheriff's snooping hadn't led to West Security and Investigations. James wasn't surprised. He had only been working for West for a few months and New York State didn't require him to have his own private investigator's license as long as a licensed private investigator supervised him. Finding a licensed PI in his family had never been a problem so he hadn't seen a reason to spend the time or money getting a license of his own. That would come in handy since the last thing he needed was the good sheriff telling Erika her new neighbor was a gumshoe.

"Just taking some downtime while I figure out my next move. Carling Lake seemed a good spot for that."

Webb nodded. "We have our fair share of tourists coming to town looking for a little R&R and to commune with nature. Some even end up setting down roots."

"I don't know about roots, but the rest, relaxation and nature sound good to me."

"Hmm."

James set his mug on the table with a thunk. "Something you want to say to me, Sheriff?"

"Don't get yourself all worked up. I was just thinking that since you're close, you might be inclined to keep an eye on Erika and Marcus. I'm not at all comfortable with today's incidents."

"Incidents, plural? I thought you were chalking Erika's fall up to an accident."

Webb frowned. "I never said that. I looked at that rope. The cut was clean just like you said. But I'm not jumping to any conclusions."

"Not jumping to any conclusions but not taking any chances, either?"

"Erika and Marcus are important to me." Webb's words elicited another stab of jealousy that James ignored. "You have a particular skill set that can be useful as their neighbor."

James's eyebrows arched. "Erika doesn't seem like a woman who'd appreciate having someone hovering over her."

"I'm not asking you to be Kevin Costner to her Whitney Houston," Webb said, eliciting a smile from James at the dated movie reference. "Just keep an eye out for them when they're home."

Since he was already doing that, there was no harm in agreeing to Webb's request.

"I'll need you to come down to the station and sign your statement. I'll call when it's ready," Webb said, rising from his seat.

James watched as Webb and Bridges got into separate cars and took off down the gravel drive.

Keep an eye out for them. Webb's voice resounded in James's head.

He planned to do more than that. Whether Erika's last name turned out to be Overholt or something else, he was going to make sure she and her son were safe.

Chapter Five

The dream was familiar, although it had been more than five years since she had it last.

Erika sat in the passenger's seat of her husband's sporty red Porsche. Roland wore a tuxedo, the bow at his neck undone. The gold beaded gown and strappy heels she had on cost more than all the clothes she'd ever owned before meeting Roland Overholt.

Roland was drunk, a state that had become common for him, and driving too fast and erratically. It was a miracle they'd made it as far as they had without getting into an accident, but it was late and thankfully the roads weren't heavily traveled.

They'd just left a party celebrating the opening of a new division of Overholt Industries. Roland had gone into the night, exuberant. He'd expected his father to appoint him to run the new division, a first step toward succeeding the old man when he retired. But Roger had passed over and humiliated both his sons by announcing his choice of one of the other senior Overholt executives for the position. Insult meet injury.

Roland dealt with the situation the way he dealt with everything, by hitting the open bar and downing whiskey until his father pulled him aside and demanded he leave.

So they'd left because Roland always did what his father told him to do. And Erika always did what Roland told her to do. She had begged Roland to pull over and let her drive, but he was lost in his head. Ranting and raving about his father underestimating him. Never believing in him. How a new division of Overholt Industries should be run by an actual Overholt.

The sound of a car horn pulled her attention from her husband's tirade. It all happened in seconds, but it felt as if they were moving in slow motion. They'd veered into the oncoming lanes. Blindingly white headlights shone through the windshield.

She looked back at Roland. His eyes had grown wide. He wrenched the steering wheel to the right but panicked, overcorrected. The Porsche sailed over the blacktop, then over the grassy patch that ran along the side of the road. The thick trunk of the tree barreled toward them and Erika heard the crunching sound of metal, tasted blood in her mouth before the world went black.

Erika started awake. She pressed a trembling hand to her chest, felt her racing heartbeat.

"Everything okay in here?" A nurse rushed into the room.

"Yes. Just a bad dream." Erika tried to smile, hoping it would soften the worried expression on the nurse's face. Her heartbeat was already slowing, and after taking her blood pressure, the nurse deemed her well enough to be left alone again.

Erika padded into the bathroom and got into the shower.

She was more than well enough to be left alone. She was thriving, and she was doing so using her smarts and grit despite all the times Roland had told her she wouldn't survive without him. She'd done more than survive.

Ten years after the car accident that took Roland's life, it was almost as if Erika Overholt was herself a dream. That the woman she was now had ever believed Roland when he'd said she was nothing without him was almost laughable. He'd tried his best to make her nothing. He'd belittled her and undermined her confidence at every turn. Nothing she'd done was good enough. *Why did you let the gardeners plant gardenias? Are you trying to embarrass me in front of the entire neighborhood? Why did you have this room painted that color? I feel like I live in a bordello. Why did you buy that dress? Everyone will think I married a streetwalker.* There was nothing too small to escape his criticism. Piece by piece, he chipped away at her. He hadn't seen her as her own person. Everything she did reflected on him. And nothing was never good enough for Roland Overholt.

They'd been married five years at the time of the accident, and the happiest moment in her marriage was when the doctor told her Roland hadn't made it.

For the briefest of moments, she'd been relieved.

Then the doctor had given her another piece of news that had sent fear like she'd never known before coursing through her. She was pregnant.

She'd been released from the hospital only to find Roger Overholt and his attorney in her home. None of the Overholts had bothered to visit her in the hospital, and she hadn't expected Roger's sudden appearance to portend good things.

She'd been right.

It turned out she and Roland didn't own the house they'd been living in. She'd naively allowed Roland to handle all their financial affairs. The house, the cars, the bank accounts. None of it was Roland's, which meant none of it was hers.

All she'd get was a hundred thousand dollars from a life insurance policy that Roger couldn't cut her out of per California law. It wasn't nothing, but for a woman who'd spent the past five years married to the millionaire son of a billionaire, it may as well have been.

Her father-in-law gave her five hours to pack her bags under the watchful eye of his attorney and left.

That night, lying sleepless in her hotel room, unsure where to go or how she'd feed the life growing inside her, she'd let herself consider, just for a moment, whether she should have let Roger know about his grandchild. The Overholt bloodline meant everything to Roger and even though he treated his two sons like dirt, that was better than he treated everyone else, as long as they submitted to his will. When they didn't, Roger made sure they paid for it. The one Overholt who'd slipped through Roger's grasp, his daughter, Daisy, had been cut off and banished from the family. Erika hadn't ever even met the woman, only hearing about her during one of Roland's drunken rants.

Erika thought back to all the times that Roland had belittled her in front of his family. How Roger had looked on, almost with pride, as if his son bullying his wife was something to be proud of. If Roger had known she was carrying an Overholt, he'd have made sure that he had control over the baby's entire life. Roger would do his best to turn her child into him.

She'd vowed then and there she wouldn't allow it. And she hadn't.

She pushed thoughts of Roger Overholt from her mind as she dressed. The Overholts weren't part of her and Marcus's lives, and they never would be.

At just past nine o'clock, Dr. Lucas Blackwell, the attending physician who'd seen her when she'd been admitted to the hospital yesterday, bustled into the room with a tablet in one hand and his stethoscope looped around his neck. "Well, aren't you an early riser? How are you feeling this morning, Ms. Powell?" He set the tablet on the bed next to her and with practiced efficiency grabbed the blood pressure cuff from the wall mount at the head of the bed and wrapped it around Erika's right arm.

"I feel fine. Ready to go home," Erika answered, forcing a smile.

They both fell silent while he worked.

"On a scale from one to ten, ten being the worst, how would you rate the pain?" he asked as he took his stethoscope from his ears and pulled the cuff from her arm.

"Two." Erika ignored the repeated pounding in her head that marked her answer as a lie.

Dr. Blackwell glanced up from the tablet he was using to record her vitals, his expression reflecting his skepticism.

He held her gaze, letting the silence stretch between them.

"Okay, it's more like a six. But a manageable six," she tacked on quickly.

The doctor nodded and went back to making notes. "I'll have the nurse bring you something for the pain when she brings in your discharge papers. It's just extra strength acetaminophen, but it will also help with the body aches."

The combined headache and body soreness was probably closer to an eight, but there was no way she was going to admit it. She had no intention of spending another night in the hospital. She'd spoken to Marcus on the phone last night. The fear and concern she heard in his voice had twisted her heart. She'd tried to assure him she was fine and that staying overnight at the hospital was only a precaution, but the best thing she could do for both of them was to get home.

Dr. Blackwell poked and prodded a bit more before announcing she was free to go, provided she took it easy for the next few days. Erika readily agreed, and he left to print her discharge papers.

She eased off the bed and went to the small closet in the room. The black coat she'd been wearing when she'd fallen hung inside next to her shirt. She had hope that a good scrubbing would get the bloodstains out of the coat, but her shirt was a lost cause. The EMTs had cut it off on the way to the hospital and only the pieces remained. Someone, one of the nurses no doubt, had left a scrub top in the closet and she'd put it and her dirt encrusted jeans on after her shower.

She grabbed her coat, tossed the shirt in the garbage and hobbled back to the bed.

Lance's questions about the bridge's maintenance and her fall had been running through her head since he'd left the day before. She knew Lance said he'd look into her fall, but she wanted to take a look at the bridge rigging for herself. Her brain pounded at the thought of the walk to the bluff.

Maybe not right away. But in a few days, when the headache had subsided, she'd take a walk out to the bluff. She was responsible for the maintenance of her property after all, and if the bridge collapse wasn't an act of nature…

She wouldn't let herself go there yet. She and Marcus had been safe in Carling Lake for the last eight years, and there was no reason to think that they weren't so any longer.

But if the Overholts had found them?

They'd run again. And this time she'd make sure they'd never be found.

Chapter Six

A knock on the room's door jerked her out of her thoughts.

James West's broad frame nearly filled the doorway. She wasn't a small woman at five foot ten, but Ronald had been several inches taller than her, and even all these years after his death, physically imposing men usually initiated her defenses. But there was something about James West, a gentleness in his eyes, that kept her walls from immediately going up.

"Sorry, I didn't mean to startle you," James said, coming farther into the room.

"No apology necessary. I was just...lost in thought."

"How are you feeling?" he asked, flashing a smile that made her heart race. Thank goodness she was no longer on a machine, or he'd know exactly how his presence affected her.

"I'll live. Right now I just want to get home and see my son."

"I spoke to Sheriff Webb this morning. He said

his deputy will drop Marcus off at school and pick him up this afternoon and bring him home."

Erika narrowed her eyes. "Why'd you have to speak to Lance this morning?"

James's smile fell away. "There was a situation at your house last night. The sheriff came out, everything is okay, but I called him this morning to follow up."

She was about to demand details when the nurse returned with her discharge papers and the pain medication Dr. Blackwell had ordered. An orderly followed, pushing a wheelchair. The nurse reminded her to take it easy until her headache went away before exiting the room again. James helped her into her coat, and the orderly pushed her through the winding hallways, James marching dutifully at her side, to the front entrance of the hospital.

They made their way slowly to the shiny black and chrome SUV Erika had seen parked in front of the small cabin next to her property for the last several days.

James took great care, settling her into the passenger seat before he climbed behind the wheel and pointed the vehicle toward home.

Erika waited until they'd turned onto the two-lane highway leading away from the hospital and back to Carling Lake before reiterating the question she'd asked back in her hospital room. "What kind of situation was there at my house last night?"

James glanced at her quickly before turning his attention back to the road ahead. "There was someone skulking around your backyard. Don't worry, I intercepted him before he made it inside."

"Is that what happened to your eye? It looks painful."

James nodded. "It's not as bad as it looks."

"Did Lance arrest the guy?" Carling Lake had its fair share of crime from pickpocketing the tourists to a growing opioid drug problem just like everywhere else in the country.

"I'm sorry. He got away."

A ripple of unease moved through her sore body.

First, the bridge collapsing and then someone trying to break into her house. Had she been found? Had Roger Overholt found her and Marcus?

The once familiar swell of panic rose in her throat, but she pushed it back down.

Don't overreact.

Erika Overholt had ceased to exist ten years ago. Erika Powell had hidden her trail well, using part of the life insurance payout to purchase a black market identity. She and Marcus were safe. Her father-in-law had been quick to kick her to the curb after Roland's death but if he knew he had a grandson, another Overholt heir, she was sure he'd stop at nothing to get Marcus under his thumb. Just as his two sons had been for their entire lives.

"You okay over there?" James eyed her from the driver's seat.

"Yes," she said, pulling herself back into the present. The pain medicine the doctor had given her had kicked in. Her headache was gone and her limbs no longer felt like lead. "Thank you for watching out for the house last night."

"Not a problem. I just wish I'd caught him."

"Well, I'm sure Lance is on top of it."

She tried not to be too conspicuous as she studied the man driving her home. His sleek black leather jacket was completely inadequate for the cold that wafted off the lake, but it certainly gave off a dangerous, sexy vibe. Jeans hugged his strong thighs, upping the sexy to nearly off-the-chart levels. Even his purplish black eye was doing it for her.

Erika bit her bottom lip and looked away before he realized she'd been ogling him.

She couldn't help the very feminine reaction she found herself having to his presence, but knew she couldn't, wouldn't, let it go anywhere. He was just passing through. She knew some of the young singles who lived in and around Carling Lake were happy to engage in temporary flings with the tourists and she didn't judge. To each their own. But casual dating had never worked for her.

Lately, dating of any fashion hadn't been working for her. It wouldn't be fair. She'd never be able to be completely honest with a partner, so what kind of relationship could she really ever have? None. She'd reconciled herself to that fact long ago. It didn't mean she wanted to live her life alone, just that she didn't have any other choice. But if she did?

Maybe she'd have given James West a chance. She could do worse than a man who'd ferry a neighbor he barely knew home from the hospital.

Yeah, why would he do that? a voice in the back of her head intoned.

After years of being careful about who she let get close to her and Marcus, she couldn't stop the little slivers of suspicion that crept into her mind anytime she met a new person. But she pushed the doubt away. What was the point of having created a new life if she couldn't trust a little? Romance may not be in the cards, but surely a ride from a neighbor wasn't dangerous. At least not to anything except her libido.

"Have you lived in Carling Lake long?" James asked. They were stopped at a traffic light, and he'd caught her ogling him like a teenaged schoolgirl.

She cleared her throat and focused her gaze out the front window of the SUV. "About eight years now." The signal changed, and he put the car in gear.

"And you have a son? How old is he?"

She smiled at the thought of her son. "Marcus. He's ten going on thirty. Do you have kids?"

"No. I haven't really stayed in one place long enough to find a woman I'd like to be a mother to my kids."

The knowledge that he wasn't forever tied to another woman in that way made her slightly giddy, although she knew she had no right to be.

"But you live in New York now?" she asked, with the intention of putting her thoughts back on neutral ground. At his questioning look, she added, "Your license plate."

He nodded. "Born and raised New Yorker, actually. I enlisted in the Marines when I was twenty but I've been out of the service for a few months now."

Something about the way he said it made her think that he wasn't exactly happy about his separation from the military but he didn't give her the chance to inquire further. "How about you? Are you from Carling Lake?"

"No," she answered without elaboration. "Where'd you serve?"

He shot a glance across the car that let her know he hadn't missed the shift back to his life as the topic. "Mostly Afghanistan, although I've seen quite a bit of the world."

"That must have been nice. Seeing the world, that is."

"It had its moments. You don't travel much?"

She laughed. "Try not at all. Between work and Marcus, I don't have a lot of free time or money for travel."

"I can understand that. My father raised four sons pretty much on his own. There wasn't a lot of money for traveling then, either. You mentioned you're about to open your home as a B&B. Running a B&B, is that what you did before you moved to Carling Lake?"

She narrowed her eyes at him, suspicion creating a knot in her belly.

Was it her imagination, or was he fishing for information about her past?

"No. I pretty much just went from one job to another before I moved here."

"A jack-of-all-trades. That will probably come in handy for an innkeeper," he said with a smile.

"I hope so," she said, forcing herself to relax. He was just making conversation. A nice guy doing the neighborly thing, giving her a ride home. "I'm actually a staff writer for the *Carling Lake Weekly*. At least I am for another few weeks. Once the B&B opens, I'll be running it full-time."

"You really do have a lot on your plate. Mom. Journalist. Businesswoman."

Erika felt her body warm at the admiration in the glance James shot her from the other side of the car. "So you've been in Carling Lake for almost a week now. How do you like it?" she asked, hoping to turn the conversation in a direction that would stop the butterflies fluttering in her stomach.

This is what comes of not having been on a date in longer than you can remember, she admonished herself. *You get all fluttery around the first good-looking guy to swing through town.*

"It's nice. Much quieter than New York City but quiet is more my speed, anyway."

"Have you taken advantage of any of the town's amenities? We've got great hiking trails and there are several things you can do at the lake, fishing, paddleboat, even a booze cruise. There's a lot to do besides jog, although I can't say I mind the view."

She couldn't believe she'd actually said that. Her mouth had obviously been moving faster than her brain. The doctor said she didn't have a concussion, but she had to wonder if he'd gotten it wrong. At least then she'd have an excuse for flirting with a man she hardly knew.

James's lips curved into a smile. "Happy to be of service."

She faced forward and prayed she wouldn't die of embarrassment. Maybe a fling was in order— not with James West of course, but clearly the lack of male companionship was causing her to lose the ability to talk to a man.

James turned the SUV onto the private road that her B&B and his cabin shared.

A familiar white F-150 was parked in the wide driveway in front of the B&B.

James frowned at the truck. "Expecting company?"

"It's okay. That's my contractor. I'm glad to see him here. He's been MIA the last few days."

Samuel Hogan was one of the most sought after contractors in Carling Lake, although that was admittedly not a difficult distinction to earn in a small town. Erika had been ecstatic when his bid for the part of the renovations she wasn't equipped to DIY had come in under her budget.

Unfortunately, their business relationship had gone downhill in the last several weeks. Hogan was two weeks late getting started with the work, and it was taking much more time than he'd originally told her it would take to finish. Even now, he was the only truck parked in the driveway, signaling the crew of five guys that had been working on the house last week weren't there with him.

She'd been conservative in her budgeting and scheduling, but if Hogan didn't step things up, the renovations wouldn't be finished in time for her to petition for the certificate of occupancy she'd need to open for the start of the tourist season.

Sam Hogan rounded the side of the house as James helped Erika from the SUV. He carried a large, battered toolbox in one hand, held the keys to his truck in the other and sported a deer-in-the-headlights expression when he caught sight of Erika and James approaching.

"Mr. Hogan. Sam. I'm glad to see you," Erika said, rounding the front of the SUV and stopping next to Sam's truck.

Sam gave her a tight smile and hoisted the toolbox into the back of his truck. "Ms. Powell, I heard about your fall. Glad to see you're feeling better."

"Thank you, Sam. I'm glad to see you. There's still a lot that needs to get done before the B&B will be approved for occupancy," Erika continued, trying to keep her tone cordial. "I hope you aren't leaving."

Sam ran his hands through his thinning hair. "I'm sorry, Erika. I'm not going to be able to finish your job. Not on your schedule, anyway."

Erika fought to keep her cool. "Not just my schedule. The schedule we agreed upon in the contract we both signed."

Sam dropped his gaze and shifted from foot to foot. "I'm sorry, but you see, I got a line on this job. It's a big one and well…it's just with things being so tight and all, I just can't say no. This could be the job that rockets my company to the next level."

"I can't see how it could be good for your company when people hear how you've abandoned a client mid-project." James crossed his arms over his chest and eyed Sam.

Sam's gaze swung up and locked onto James, his eyes narrowing. "I don't remember anyone asking for your opinion. Who are you, anyway?"

"You'd better hope I'm not a potential customer," James answered.

Sam swallowed hard.

Erika drew in a deep breath and held her hands up in a stop motion. "Sam, this is unacceptable. We have a contract. You're already behind schedule. I can't afford any more delays."

"And I can't afford not to take this other job. All of your big projects are done. It'll take me four or five months but I can get back to your job after I've finished this one. Or if you want to look for another contractor, I'm willing to take what you've already paid me and void the rest of the contract. You could probably even go with a handyman for what's left. Whichever works for you."

"What works for me is for you to hold up your end of our deal." Erika fought against frustration to keep herself from yelling at the contractor. "What is this other job, anyway? I don't know of any big projects taking place in Carling Lake right now."

It was quite the opposite. For the last two or three years, the town had been suffering from a decline in tourist dollars that had left the city coffers lighter than in past years. The last several city council member meetings had been focused on reinvigorating the flow of tourists to the town.

"It came up kind of sudden." Sam was back to shifting his feet.

Erika got the feeling that she was not going to like whatever he was about to say.

"Ellis Hanes is looking to renovate a wing of the hotel. He wants the project done in time for the tourist season." Sam's face turned the color of a ripe tomato. At least he had enough character to be ashamed of leaving her in the lurch.

Of course, Ellis was behind this. Another attempt to run her out of business before she even got started.

"Look, this isn't just about me. A renovated hotel will help with bringing in more tourists. The whole town will benefit."

"My B&B will bring in more tourists as well, also benefiting the town," Erika gritted out.

Sam wrenched open the truck's driver's side door. "I'm sorry, Erika. My decision is made." He hopped into the truck and started the engine. Sam wound his window down until he could hang an arm out and pat the side of the door. "Let me know what you decide about the work here. Like I said, either way is fine with me."

Sam threw the truck in reverse and roared off without giving her the chance to respond. "What am I going to do? If I don't get these renovations done soon, there's no way I'll have my occupancy permit in time for my spring and summer bookings."

"Maybe I could help."

"You have your contractor's license?"

"No, but my father taught all his sons to be handy, and I've been helping my brother Ryan renovate the house he bought for his family. As long as your contractor wasn't lying about the big projects being done, I can probably handle it."

It was better for a lot of reasons if she kept her distance from him and he from her. "I couldn't ask you to do that. I mean, you said you were here for rest and relaxation. Becoming my handyman is hardly a restful vacation."

He cocked his head. "That's a matter of perspective." He gave her another one of his brilliant smiles.

"Thank you, but no. I appreciate the ride from the hospital." She turned and headed for the house.

"Here, let me help you."

Erika held up a hand to stop him from moving any closer. "No, really. I've got it from here. Enjoy your vacation, Mr. West."

Chapter Seven

"There's something strange going on here." James spoke to Ryan using the hands-free setting in the SUV as he made the short drive from his cabin into downtown Carling Lake for the second time that day.

On his way out, he'd seen Erika dragging her trash bin to the edge of her property. He'd been about to rush over to help when a preteen boy sprinted down the porch steps and took the bins from her hands. Good. At least someone was looking out for the stubborn woman. Erika may not have a concussion, but a head wound was nothing to take lightly. She should have been resting.

You're here to do a job, not play nursemaid.

That might be true, but it didn't stop the protective impulses that seemed to flare whenever Erika got within his eyesight. Maybe it was just compensatory guilt because he felt bad about lying to her, about why he was actually in Carling Lake. But the fluttering he'd felt as she sat beside him in the SUV on the way home from the hospital whispered that guilt wasn't the emotion that was stirring his loins.

"Weird how?" Ryan's concerned voice pulled James out of his head.

"Yesterday morning a bridge gave out while Erika was on it. Then while she was in the hospital someone tried to break into her house." James filled in a few more details for Ryan.

"I'll admit the lady had a tough day, but it sounds like the local sheriff is on top of it. I don't see how it affects the job you're there to do," Ryan said.

"You don't think it's fishy that we're hired to find Erika Overholt and then she just happens to fall from a bridge and almost have her home broken into?"

James just couldn't shake the feeling that something about this case was wrong. If Erika Powell really was Erika Overholt, she'd gone to extremes to hide her identity. Why?

West's research into the Overholt family had turned up not-so-veiled insinuations by the family members that Erika may have had something to do with her husband's accident, but the police reports were unequivocal. Erika's husband's car had slid off the road during a heavy rainstorm and slammed into a tree, killing him. The toxicology report had put his blood alcohol level at well above the legal limit. The Overholts may not agree, but it was a miracle that Erika hadn't also been killed that night.

So why all the subterfuge on Erika's part?

"I just don't understand why all the secrecy. If the woman I'm watching is Erika Overholt, she's been hiding who she is for years. And now the executors of Overholt's will are asking us to keep secrets. None of it sits right with me."

"According to Overholt's attorney, the will specifically requires that the grandson and daughter-in-law be found and their identities confirmed before they are told of any behests. Actually, all the heirs have to be told about their inheritance at the same time and place. Apparently, Overholt was controlling and eccentric until his last breath."

"And beyond," James sighed.

"We've been hired to do a job."

"And asking questions is part of that job." His statement elicited a groan from the other end of the line. "Look, I'm going to do what you sent me up here to do but it can't hurt if I poke around."

Ryan was right that they'd been hired simply to find Erika Overholt and her son. Once they did, the attorneys for Roger Overholt's estate would take it from there. If Erika didn't want the inheritance, wanted to continue to live under the radar as Erika Powell, she could. He wasn't doing anything wrong.

Then why didn't it feel right?

"Whatever, man. Just don't let your poking around interfere with the case. The attorney for the executor of Overholt's will is expecting results soon. It's already taken us longer to find this woman than we'd hoped."

Over the last two months, West Security and Investigations had run down several leads that had only led to dead ends. Erika Overholt had disappeared off the map—not easy to do in this day and age. James wasn't even totally sure how Ryan had finally been able to track her down. His brother was good at what he did, he'd give him that.

"I thought I'd figured out a way into the house but it turned out to be a dead end."

"How so?" Ryan asked.

"Erika's converting her house into a B&B. Her contractor quit on her unexpectedly. I offered to help out, but she shut me down cold."

"That's too bad," Ryan said, sounding disappointed. "If there's anything that can prove Erika Powell's identity, it's in there."

"I'll figure something out."

"I have faith in you." Ryan fell silent for a moment. "How's the second part of your mission coming?"

"I don't know if I'd call it a mission."

"I would. In your downtime, you're supposed to be camping and fishing and whatever else you outdoorsy types do in the woods. And most importantly, figuring out what your next steps are going to be after the military."

"I plan to do all that *outdoorsy* stuff as soon as I've finished this job. As for the rest of it…"

"Look, you know you can work for the firm as long as you like. Hell, you're entitled to a fourth of the business."

James West Sr. had left the business to all four of his sons in equal shares when he'd retired. At the time, James had had no intention of leaving the military and his next oldest brother, Brandon, had just embarked on a promising legal career. They'd both sold their interest in the family business to their two youngest brothers.

"No. You and Shawn have done a great job turning West into a first-class security and investigations firm. You deserve to own and run the business. I may not be sure what I want my post–Marine Corps life to be but I don't think private investigations and personal security is for me."

"Well, just know that whatever you decide, you've got my support."

"Thanks, man."

They ended the call as James pulled into the parking lot next to the Lakeside Diner. The lunch rush had subsided and the diner's only other customer was a sole male sitting at the counter. James selected a table against the wall and sat so he could see the entrance.

A server with the name Kelly embroidered on her uniform bounded over to his table. She flashed a sultry smile and poured water into his glass from the pitcher she carried. "Welcome to the Lakeside Diner. What can I get you, something special today?" The tone of her voice made it clear she was talking about more than lunch, but just in case he'd missed it, Kelly shot him a wink.

The door to the diner opened and James made eye contact with the sheriff. He turned back to Kelly, purposely keeping his expression bland. "Burger and fries, please," he said, nestling the laminated menu back between the salt and pepper shakers on the table.

Kelly's smile dimmed. She scratched his order on her pad and turned away from the table.

"I'll have whatever he's having." Lance slid into the chair on the opposite side of the table.

Kelly poured Lance a glass of water before leaving to put in their order.

"Make yourself comfortable," James said.

"Don't mind if I do," Lance smiled. "This isn't New York City. You want to eat alone, you don't come to the diner."

"I have no problem with company," James countered.

"I talked to Erika last night. Thank you for making sure she got home alright."

"It's not a problem. Despite what you might have heard, we New Yorkers can be neighborly, too."

Lance chuckled. "You know I haven't always been the sheriff. Before I moved to Carling Lake, I did an eight-year stint as an officer in the Atlanta Police Department."

"Atlanta. That's a long way from Carling Lake."

"That was the point." Lance's expression hardened for the briefest of moments before it evened out. "We got a print off the kerosene can we found at Erika's last night."

"That was quick."

"We run prints in-house. The fingerprint came back to a Brian Whitmer. I recognized the name. He's one of several regulars who show up at the start of the tourist season to take on seasonal work for the businesses in town. So far no one knows where he is."

"He's probably gone by now."

Lance sighed. "Yeah, I figured that. I put out an all-points bulletin but with no fixed address and no description of a vehicle, it may take some time to run him to ground."

"Anything on the rope from the bridge yet?" James asked.

Lance shook his head. "That I had to send to the county lab. It may be a few days. If we're lucky."

"Here you are. Two burgers with fries." Kelly returned and set a plate in front of each of them.

"Thanks."

"Thank you," James seconded.

Lance must have been as starved as James because he dug in the minute Kelly walked away from the table. James followed suit.

"Carling Lake doesn't get many marine snipers passing through town," Lance said after he'd finished half the food on his plate.

"Former sniper," James said, washing a handful of fries down with a sip of water.

Lance wiped ketchup from his mouth. "Why'd you leave the service?"

James cocked an eyebrow. "You don't already know?"

"I only checked your criminal record to make sure Erika and Marcus weren't in any danger with you next door. The rest of the story is yours to tell."

James took a long sip of water, eyeing Lance over the rim of the mug.

"Or not." Lance shrugged.

James waited several more beats before speaking. "There was a suicide bomber on my last tour in Afghanistan about a year ago. I was a good distance away, which probably saved my life, but a piece of shrapnel still found me. Tore through my hand, damaging tendons."

"I'm sorry to hear that, truly." Lance's voice rang with sincerity.

"Thanks. With lots of therapy, I've got what the doctors call *normal function* back."

"But normal function isn't enough for a sniper."

"No, it is not."

"It's probably enough for a sheriff's deputy."

James felt the corner of his mouth creep upward. "Are you making an offer?"

"One of my deputies just got engaged and is moving to North Carolina in the coming weeks to be with his fiancée. I'll be looking for another deputy."

"Do you make job offers to every tourist who comes to town?"

"Just the special ones." Lance grinned. "What have you been doing since you left the service? I mean job-wise."

He didn't want to lie, but he couldn't tell the truth, either. "A little bit of this. A little bit of that."

"Okay, but you're what? Thirty-six, thirty-seven. You can't do *a little bit of this and a little bit of that* for the next twenty years."

"You sound like my brother," James deadpanned.

"So what are your plans?"

James glared across the table. "I'm still working on that."

"Lots of vets go into law enforcement," Lance said pointedly.

James arched an eyebrow. "I don't think it's for me."

"Because of your hand?"

James stayed silent.

They ate in silence for several minutes.

Lance swallowed the last bite of his burger. "Do you have anywhere to be?"

James shot Lance a questioning look. "Not particularly."

"Good. Come on. You can leave your car here. I'll drive." Lance rose, dropped enough money to cover the entire bill on the table and headed for the exit.

James considered for a moment. He wasn't sure getting too friendly with the sheriff was a good idea. Lance was bound to be upset if he learned James had been lying since his first moments in town. But he was curious about what the sheriff had in mind. He pushed up from the table and followed Lance out of the diner.

James closed the door on the passenger side of the sheriff's cruiser as Lance started the engine.

Lance filled him in on the people, sights and scenery they passed as he drove.

James wasn't sure why, but he mentally cataloged

each turn, drawing a map of the town in his head as they drove.

Fifteen minutes after leaving the diner, Lance hit his left-turn signal and coasted into the parking lot of a single-story cinder block building on the outskirts of town.

Lance parked, climbed out of the car and headed for the building without a word.

James followed, almost missing the small sign to the right of the door. Precision Gun Range.

A short man, not much more than a foot taller than the glass case he stood behind, with a beer belly and only a handful of gray strands failing miserably at covering the bald spot at the top of his head, looked up as they entered.

The man broke into a wide smile at the sight of Lance. "Been a while, Sheriff. Come to let me show you up again?"

"Not today, Ari. My friend here and I want to get some target practice in."

Ari's gaze shifted to James. Up close, James could see that the man was at least twenty years older than he and Lance, but the light in his eyes was bright. "Who is your friend, and does he know how to shoot?"

James slanted the older man a look, but Lance only chuckled. "I'll say he does. Ari Levy meet Master Sergeant James West, US Marine Corps."

James reached across the glass case and shook Ari's hand. The older man gave him a thorough once-over.

"Guess I don't have to worry about you accidentally shooting yourself in the foot, then."

"No, sir, you don't," James said, finding the older man growing on him despite his surly personality.

"James was a sniper," Lance added.

"Good for you." The older man didn't appear impressed. "Well then, can I load you up?"

"Yes, please. This was a last-minute idea so we'll need the works. Ammo, ear and eye protection, and a gun for my friend."

"You got a preference?" Ari asked, collecting the items they'd need and setting them on the counter.

"That a SIG?" James jerked his chin at the gun on Lance's hip.

"P226," Lance said, reciting the model of the gun.

Ari reached into the glass case and extracted a gun in a holster that looked exactly like the one Lance wore. "Slow day, so I won't charge you for the space. Send the bill to the sheriff's department?"

"You can send it to the department but make it to my attention," Lance answered. "This one is on me."

"Gotcha." Ari made an air gun with his finger. "Lanes are ready to go. Have fun, boys."

James and Lance gathered their equipment and James followed the sheriff through a heavy metal door. The smell of gunpowder filled James's nose the moment he crossed the threshold.

"Your friend is a character." James sat his gear on the counter in the lane closest to the door. Lance took the next lane.

"Don't let him fool you. Ari might not be a marine sharpshooter but he's a damn good shot."

Lance disappeared behind the divider separating them. James put on his safety goggles and ear protection and loaded his gun with target ammo. He could hear Lance on the other side of the divider going through the same routine.

James took a deep breath, pulling the trigger as he exhaled. His shot missed the mark wildly, leaving a hole in the white space next to the dark silhouette on the paper. He adjusted and took another shot. Better. But his hand was already trembling.

This time he'd hit the target, but nowhere near the bull's-eye. The sound of his blood thundered in his ears. He could feel his body tensing with swelling anxiety.

He took another deep breath, clenched his right hand more firmly with his left in an attempt to stop the trembling and emptied the clip.

Each shot was better than the one before, and all of them had hit the target in an area that would have been debilitating to an actual person, but nowhere near as good as he'd once been. Beads of sweat collected on his forehead by the time he'd empty the clip, as much from frustration as from the exertion of trying to hold his hand steady.

He ejected the empty magazine and set the gun on the counter.

Lance stepped around the divider and removed his earmuffs. "You're not that bad. Not bad at all."

James also removed his earmuffs. "Not bad isn't good."

"You'd more than pass the firearms test."

"Law enforcement isn't for me."

Lance pulled the protective glasses from his eyes. "Look, I barely know you so maybe I'm overstepping my bounds here but I have friends who have left the military and found the transition…difficult." Lance placed a hand on James's shoulder. "If you want to talk, I'm a good listener and even better at keeping what I hear to myself."

James waited for Lance to return to his lane, then dropped his protection goggles back over his eyes. He still didn't think law enforcement was for him, but the people of Carling Lake were definitely growing on him.

Chapter Eight

The third contractor of the morning was politely laughing Erika off the phone when the banging at her front door started. She peeked around the wall separating the kitchen from the foyer and through the side windows, and saw Daisy standing on her porch.

"The best I could do for you is to have someone out there in late May," the contractor on the other end of the phone line said as Erika opened the door to let Daisy in.

"Thanks anyway," Erika replied before ending the call.

"I bought you dinner for tonight and some staples that should keep you for a few days. What are you doing out of bed?" Daisy breezed through the front door and into the kitchen, a casserole dish in her hands and a recyclable shopping bag hanging from her arm.

"Thank you, but you didn't have to do that. I'm fine. I rested all day yesterday. And most of the morning. Steven Sanchez offered to take Marcus to school for the rest of this week."

Erika made a mental note to thank Devin's fathers for everything they'd done for her over the last several days and followed Daisy into the kitchen. "I have to find a contractor to finish the work on the house."

"Ugh." Daisy made a face. "I heard Sam left you in the lurch." She put the casserole in the refrigerator and set the grocery bag on the island counter. "I thought he had more integrity than that."

So had Erika. She'd known Sam for the last eight years, ever since she'd moved to Carling Lake, and she'd heard nothing but great things about him and his work. He'd done the heavy lifting on renovating the kitchen three years ago when she'd purchased the house. "Ellis has a lot of influence and deeper pockets than I do. No one wants to run afoul of him."

Daisy slammed a loaf of bread onto the counter. "That doesn't excuse Sam. He had a contract with you and he should have kept his word and done the job he'd agreed to do."

Erika grabbed a jar of peanut butter and a box of ready-made pancake mix and walked to the pantry. "I'm not disagreeing with you but I can't make him do the work so I have to find someone who will."

"Any luck?"

Erika's gaze traveled to the window. She'd glimpsed James this morning out on his porch. She'd spent the night feeling guilty for how dismissive she'd been of his offer to help with the renovations. He was only being nice, neighborly. Which had instantly aroused her suspicions. But maybe she was letting her general mistrust of people cloud her judgment. "No."

Daisy braced herself against the counter. "Okay, give," she said with interest in her eyes.

"Give what?" Erika worked to wipe whatever Daisy had seen in her expression from her face.

"Why did you just shoot a longing look out the window at your gorgeous neighbor's cabin?"

Erika rolled her eyes. "I didn't shoot a longing look anywhere." Daisy stared. "I may have glanced out the window." Daisy continued staring through narrowed eyes. "Okay, James was here when Sam quit and he offered to help me finish the renovations."

"That's awfully nice of him," Daisy said, eyebrows wagging suggestively.

"What are you, twelve? Come on." Erika gave her friend a good-natured shoulder bump. "He's a complete stranger. I said no."

"Why? You need help. He can help. How much do you need to know about the man who's installing a toilet for you?"

When Daisy laid it out that way, it did seem like she might be being a bit overcautious.

Erika pushed away from the counter and grabbed the electric teapot, filling it with water before setting it to boil.

"And maybe he'd be willing to do a little renovation on your love life." Daisy slid out of the way when Erika went to shoulder bump her again. "Come on. I've lived here for a year and you haven't gone out on one date in that time. I wouldn't be surprised to learn you haven't been on a date since you moved to Carling Lake."

"Now that's not true. I have been on a date in the last eight years."

A few years after she'd moved to Carling Lake, she'd briefly dated a man who was also new to the area. Unfortunately, he found the mountain air and small town did not work with his city sensibilities and had moved back to the West Coast after a few months.

"Okay, but how long ago was that?" Daisy didn't wait for Erika to answer. "From the way James was looking at you in the hospital, he'd totally go for it. There is definitely chemistry between the two of you."

"There is no chemistry. And he's a tourist." *Liar.* She recalled the butterflies in her stomach when he'd driven her home. She was attracted to James West. Erika reached into the cabinet for two teacups.

"Which makes him perfect for your purposes. You can ease back into the dating game, no pressure, no long-term expectations. Just some good old-fashioned adult fun." Daisy wiggled her eyebrows.

"Daisy!"

But now that Daisy had placed the idea in her head, she wondered if that was why James had offered to help her with her house? He had to have some reason for making the offer, right? Had he assumed the small-town single mom would be open to a fling?

"What? I'm talking about dinner, maybe dancing." Daisy tried for an innocent expression and failed. "What did you think I was talking about?" Daisy couldn't keep the laughter out of her voice and Erika found herself laughing along with her friend.

"Look, I am not interested in a man at this point in my life," Erika said, carrying her tea to the kitchen table and sitting.

Daisy followed with her own cup. "Remember a couple of days ago when you and I were at the coffee shop in town and James jogged by. Your eyes nearly popped out of your head."

"It's February in New York and he was out jogging in a sleeveless T-shirt and shorts. Anybody would have stared. I was merely concerned that the man was going to get hypothermia," Daisy said, fanning herself dramatically.

"That man is too hot to ever have to worry about hypothermia."

"Ah, you are incorrigible. Okay, I will admit, he's hot. I shamelessly ogled all those rippling muscles as he jogged past. Are you happy now?"

"Thrilled!" Daisy said, clapping.

"This changes nothing. I'm not getting involved with a tourist."

"But you should let him help you with the renovations." Daisy held up a hand when Erika opened her mouth to protest. "It's the only way you'll get done in time to file the occupancy papers and get the permit before March, and you know it."

"I have a few more contractors to call. Maybe

one of them has had a job fall through or is in a slow period."

Daisy's expression was doubtful.

Erika glanced at her watch. "Hey, I don't mean to rush you out but I want to stop by the *Weekly* before I pick up Marcus."

"Do you not understand the words *take it easy*?"

She knew her friend was just watching out for her, but Daisy's tone still grated. "I do, but I also have a job to do. And it's not like checking in and going through my email is taxing work."

At the front door, Daisy pulled her into a hug. "Call if you need anything." Letting go, Daisy bounded out the door and down the porch steps before turning back. "And think about letting your hot neighbor help you with your renovations. All your renovations," her friend said, laughing as she hopped into her car and drove away.

Thirty minutes later, Erika walked into the lobby of the *Carling Lake Weekly* and was unsurprised to find the reception desk empty. She worked as a part-time reporter. The *Weekly*'s other two employees were the owners Aaron and Margaret Sutton. Everyone in town knew to go right up to the second floor if they had business at the *Weekly*.

Erika moved through the lobby, casting only a passing glance at the framed front pages decorating the walls. Beyond the lobby area was the large room that housed the printers. The *Weekly* was one of the only local newspapers that still maintained its own printing facilities. The Suttons supplemented the income the *Weekly* brought in by handling the printing for several of the surrounding towns' weekly newspapers as well.

The second floor was set up bullpen-style. The three employee desks sat in a loose circle about six feet apart from one another. There was a conference room in one corner of the room and a small break room in the other.

Aaron looked up from the bulky computer screen on his desk as Erika walked into the bullpen. "What are you doing here?"

"I work here." Erika quirked an eyebrow. "Unless you're trying to tell me something?"

When she'd pulled into Carling Lake eight years ago with a two-year-old in tow and relatively few references, she'd expected to have to pick up a job waitressing or manning the cash register at a fast-food joint to make ends meet. She would have been fine with that. It wouldn't have been the first time. Since leaving the Overholts two years prior, she'd not stayed in one place longer than six months. That had made it very difficult to develop a solid résumé. She'd also been too afraid that working in journalism might lead to the Overholts one day accidentally discovering where she was and that she had a son who, with each passing year, looked more and more like his father.

The only job available when she'd gone to town had been the receptionist position at the *Weekly*. She'd accepted the position. It paid a lot more than waitressing and allowed her to save toward the down payment she needed to buy the B&B and start a new dream.

From the moment she'd started working at the *Weekly*, Aaron, Margaret and their son, Francis, had taken her and Marcus into their family. Soon enough, she was feeling the itch to get back on a beat. It took over a year to convince herself that none of the Overholts would be caught dead reading a small-town paper. She'd approached Aaron about creating a part-time staff reporter position and, despite the fact that she couldn't tell him about her degree in journalism, he'd given her a chance.

"You know what I mean. Lance called Margaret and told her about your fall yesterday, although she'd already heard it through the town grapevine. We would have come by to see you but the sheriff put out the word you needed rest."

"I know. I got Margaret's voice mail and the flowers she sent were at the house when I woke up this morning."

"Why aren't you at home resting?"

"I rested all day yesterday and this morning. I need to do something."

Aaron screwed up his face. "I don't like it."

"I'm just here to check my email. See if I got any response from the federal government on my FOIA request." Erika took a seat at her desk and booted up her computer.

The Freedom of Information Act was a federal law every journalism student became intimately familiar with. Many a big story had come from combing through information the law compelled the government to turn over to an intrepid journalist.

"That could have waited another day or two," he said, surliness tinging his tone.

"But I couldn't have." She ignored Aaron's frown and scrolled through her emails.

As a twenty-something journalism student, she'd imagined a career as an investigative reporter in a big city at a nationally recognized newspaper. Then during her junior year, her mother had gotten sick. Her illness had been unexpected and had claimed her mother's life quickly. When she met Ronald, she'd been alone and deeply depressed, on her way to failing out of school. Roland had seemed like a bright light at the end of an endlessly dark tunnel. And he had been until Ronald went to work for his father's company.

She shook off those memories. That was all in the past. She enjoyed her job at the *Carling Lake Weekly*. It may not have been the *LA Times*, but she was honored to work with the Suttons and proud of how they kept the community informed of important news.

But over the years, she'd found herself entertaining the dream of running a bed-and-breakfast. Maybe it was the influence of living in a tourist town. Or maybe more than just her name had changed when she left LA. Maybe her dreams had, too. Whatever it was, she was looking forward to becoming a business owner.

There was no response to her FOIA request, but she did find an email from a familiar sender. The source had first contacted her several weeks earlier via an email with an attached letter showing the town of Carling Lake had been awarded a three-hundred-thousand-dollar grant from the feds for the restoration of city hall. Whatever message the sender was trying to convey, she hadn't gotten it.

The restoration of the historic city hall building was a constant topic at council meetings. After several years, the town had finally allocated the funds for the renovations. She had covered many of those council meetings and she couldn't remember hearing anything about the town applying for or winning a grant. She'd followed up with Susan Garraus, the treasurer, and Ellis Hanes, who served as town mayor, but they'd both claimed to know nothing about the grant. She called the federal office that had supposedly awarded the grant, but the contact person hadn't returned any of her more than a half dozen calls inquiring about the money. Hence, her as yet unanswered FOIA request.

Her reporter instincts had tingled, but without more, there was nothing for her to pursue.

Erika clicked on the new email from the source. Unlike the first email, this one included a message in addition to an attachment.

WHERE IS THE MONEY?

She opened the attached document. It was another letter, only this time the government was demanding the town provide evidence that the three-hundred-thousand-dollar grant had been used as outlined in the grant application.

Where's the money?

That was the three-hundred-thousand-dollar question. The government clearly believed it had sent the money to Carling Lake. So where was it?

Her instincts were tingling again. There was something to this, she was sure. She just had to sniff out the story.

"What are you looking at so intensely?" Aaron asked from his desk.

"Another email about the grant."

"The one that Ellis and Susan say doesn't exist."

"One and the same. Only according to this demand letter I'm looking at, the government not only thinks the money exists, they think Carling Lake has it."

Aaron stood and came around the desks. He read the letter over her shoulder. "It definitely looks like they do. And you haven't heard anything about your FOIA request."

Erika shook her head. "Only that they received it and there are responsive documents."

Aaron rubbed his chin. "I have a few reporter friends in DC. I'll call them and see if they have any contacts at the office they're willing to share with me."

"Thanks. I'm going to visit Susan again. Maybe she's turned up something since we last spoke."

Aaron's eyebrow arched. "Rest. Lance specifically said the doctor mentioned you needed rest."

Erika glanced at the clock on her computer screen. She logged out of the system and grabbed her purse, dropping a kiss on the older man's cheek as she slid past. "I've got to pick up Marcus. I'll see you later."

As EXPECTED, THE parents waiting outside Carling Lake Elementary for their kids to come running out of the school building at the sound of the dismissal bell had heard about her fall. Erika accepted the words of concern, demurred on offers of help and deflected attempts to pry the story out of her of how she'd fallen. Undoubtedly, whatever the gossip mill had dreamed up was far more entertaining than the truth, anyway.

The school bell finally rang. Erika's heart swelled to nearly bursting when she caught sight of Marcus running across the playground with his arms outstretched.

Marcus bowled into her, pushing her back into the fencing surrounding the playground yard and making her sore muscles tighten. Not that she minded a bit. Hugs from her nearly eleven-year-old son were coming fewer and further between as the years ticked by and she savored every one he willingly gave.

"How was your day? Are you still okay?" Marcus leaned back, but kept his arms around her waist. His big brown eyes emanated concern.

Her heart twisted at the worry etched on her son's face. Marcus had barely left her side the evening before, bustling about the house, making sure she was comfortable. He'd made them dinner, two peanut butter and jelly sandwiches and a salad, which had mostly just been lettuce, but he was proud of himself, so she happily ate it. He'd even let her have control over the television remote. Her son was turning into a kind, caring, self-sufficient young man and she couldn't have been prouder.

"I'm fine. You don't have to worry about me." They stood partially blocking one of the exits, parents and kids streaming around them, but Erika ignored the looks.

"I know you said you were fine, but I was still a little worried about you being on your own all day." Marcus looked up at her sheepishly.

"Now you know how I feel whenever you're out of my sight." She dropped a kiss on his forehead.

"Mooomm!" Marcus stepped from her arms, scanning the playground to see if any of his friends had seen him get a kiss from his mother.

"Come on," she said, smiling and pulling him back to her side. "I thought we could stop by Moulton's and get a couple of cones before heading home."

"Definitely!" Marcus bounced up and down with excitement. Like her, Marcus ascribed to the idea that ice cream wasn't just for the summer months.

Moulton's ice-cream parlor was only a short walk from the school. Erika left the car in its parking space and they strolled through Carling Lake's downtown area, a series of interconnecting streets that were home to a variety of shops designed to serve the needs of both the full-time residents and the tourists. A secondhand bookstore, antique and souvenir shop, and clothing store with kitschy T-shirts in its window stood side by side with the post office, a bank and the local pharmacy.

Moulton's, a town and tourist favorite, was housed in a redbrick building with an old-time awning over the door. The shop had been in operation for forty-two years according to the plaque by the register, but the building itself had stood for more than one hundred years, serving as the town's first police station. From housing prisoners to fifteen of the best flavors of homemade ice cream Erika had ever tasted—an upgrade in her humble opinion.

The shop wasn't busy. Although it was Erika's contention that ice cream never went out of season, one which Moulton's apparently agreed with since it was open all year, not everyone enjoyed ice cream in the cool temperatures of February. More for her and Marcus, who never turned down sweets.

It was a sunny day, so she and Marcus took their ice cream—raspberry crumble for Erika and blueberry blues for Marcus—to the park a half block away.

Between licks, Marcus told her about what he'd done in school that day. Unlike some parents, she never had to pull a description of his day from her son. Maybe it was because they were all each other had, but she was lucky that they were close.

Although Marcus had only paused long enough for Erika to get in a few "uh-huhs" and "that sounds fun," he still somehow managed to finish his ice-cream cone before she did. The appearance of a couple of guys he recognized from school on the basketball courts may have been a motivating factor. Marcus quickly abandoned her to eat her cone alone.

She didn't mind. She loved how independent her son was, often reminding herself that his intelligence and self-sufficiency must be a sign that she wasn't screwing him up too much in those difficult times when she doubted herself as a mother.

She was finishing the last bite of her cone and readying to signal to Marcus that it was time for them to head home when a familiar and unwelcome voice came from behind her.

"Heard you've been having a bit of trouble the last couple of days. Really sad to hear that."

Erika took a deep breath and counted to ten before turning to face Ellis. She immediately regretted it when she saw the Cheshire cat grin he wore. The rage she'd felt when Sam Hogan had admitted that he was walking off her job to take on Ellis's returned with a vengeance. She fought the urge to slap the grin off Ellis's face.

If she could have separated his character and personality from his looks, she might have found him attractive. She knew his olive-colored skin resulted from the tanning salon off Route 127 rather than any time spent outdoors and his blond hair was cut a little too long and his highlights a little too well placed to be natural. He had coal-gray eyes that many of the women in town found irresistible, which he didn't mind using to his greatest advantage. In his late forties, he was a confirmed bachelor but prolific dater.

From what she'd heard, he was generous with his girlfriends until he tired of them, which didn't take long, at which point he unceremoniously moved on.

"Hard to believe since you're the source of one of my problems."

Ellis waved away her accusation. "Ah, come on now, Erika. It's just business. Sam Hogan is the best contractor for miles and I always get the best."

Erika let her gaze travel over the impeccably cut suit and coat he wore down to the loafers, probably Italian or some other ridiculously expensive kind. Ellis's entire look screamed that he had money and wanted everyone to know it. Too bad money couldn't buy integrity.

"And you suddenly had to renovate your hotel this close to the beginning of the tourist season?"

"I moved when the numbers dictated. The way I see it, you should thank me. I taught you a valuable lesson. If you want to go head to head with me in business, you better toughen up."

She shoved her hands in her pockets to keep him from seeing that they shook with anger. She wasn't a violent person by nature, but she detested Ellis. "I don't want to have anything to do with you at all."

His eyes narrowed and his lips thinned. "That's too bad. I was going to say that I'm sure I could find a job for you at one of my properties when your B&B tanks. But of course you'd have to work on your attitude."

She stepped toward him, getting into his space.

"My attitude is just fine but if you don't like it, feel free to leave me and my attitude alone."

Ellis's sneer deepened. He opened his mouth to retort, but stopped when a deep voice spoke behind Erika.

"Is there a problem here?"

Chapter Nine

The slightly paunchy, sandy-haired man looked James up and down derisively. "Best you mind your own business. I'm talking to the lady."

James stepped closer to Erika. "Not if she doesn't want to talk to you."

Lance had just dropped James back at his car when his gaze had landed on Erika talking to a man in the park across from the diner. Based on Erika's body language, the conversation was not one she welcomed. Without considering whether she'd appreciate his intervention, and more than a little frustrated by the target practice session, he'd stalked across the street.

The man's back straightened, his chest puffing out. "Look, I don't know who you think you are but this isn't any of your business."

James dropped his gaze to Erika's face. "Is he bothering you?"

Erika's scowl deepened. "This is Ellis Hanes." Ah, now the animosity made sense. James's dislike for the man grew exponentially. "He was just sharing his unsolicited opinion that my business doesn't stand a chance and I should just give up. And I was about to explain that it will be a cold day in—"

"Got it," James said, fighting the smile that wanted to break out. A strong woman would never not be sexy. He turned back to Hanes. "You heard the woman. She doesn't want to talk to you."

"Who the blazes are you?" Ellis asked, indignation ringing in his tone.

"James West. Erika's neighbor."

"Well, neighbor. I'm the mayor of this town and this conversation doesn't concern you. We need to talk." Hanes reached out a hand to grab Erika.

Erika recoiled.

James slid in front of her, blocking Hanes and simultaneously stepping into his space. "I don't care if you're the President of the United States. The lady doesn't want to speak to you so it's in your best interest to walk away right now." James only had a few inches on Hanes, but it was enough to allow him to look down on the man.

"Or what?" Hanes's gaze was hard, but there was a tremor in his voice that signaled he knew he'd gone too far.

James leaned forward slightly, crowding Hanes even further, and lowered his voice to just above a whisper. "Leave."

Hanes took a step back, his eyes darting from Erika to James. They'd attracted the attention of a couple leaving the diner on the other side of the street. The man and woman gawked at them as if they were watching a movie unfold. They'd managed not to attract the attention of Marcus and his friends yet, but that luck would not hold if Hanes continued to press the issue.

Undoubtedly sensing he'd lost this round, Hanes took several more steps backward. "We'll continue this conversation later, Erika." Turning on his heel, Hanes stalked away.

Something about the incident didn't sit well with James. It wasn't unheard of for a less-than-ethical businessperson to attempt to keep others out of their market, but an aura of desperation hung around Hanes. And desperate people did stupid, sometimes dangerous, things.

Ellis Hanes was one man James planned to keep an eye on.

James turned to Erika, ready to apologize for jumping in where he hadn't been invited and take his licks for doing so.

"Thank you," she said before he uttered a single sound. "Ellis can be a pain and I was hoping not to create a scene in front of Marcus."

"You're welcome."

As if his mother saying his name had summoned him, Marcus jogged up to them. "Hey, Mom." Marcus eyed James with naked curiosity. "Aren't you the guy renting the cabin next to our house?"

"Marcus! Manners!" Erika admonished.

Marcus dropped his head for a moment before raising his gaze to James's and thrusting out his right hand. "I'm Marcus Powell. Pleased to meet you."

"James West. And yes, I am renting the cabin next to your house."

Marcus's eyes lit up. "Cool. Do you play basketball?" Marcus jerked his head to the now-empty court. "My friends had to leave, but we don't have to go home yet, do we, Mom?" Marcus looked to Erika for approval.

"Just a little while longer. We need to get home."

Marcus shifted his gaze back to James. "Cool, so you want to come?"

His jeans and black leather boots weren't exactly regulation attire, but the way Marcus was looking at him made it impossible to say no to the kid. "Sure. It's been a while since I've been on a basketball court though so go easy on me."

The rapid shift in mood was a little disconcerting. A minute ago, he'd been running off a belligerent Ellis Hanes and now he was engaged in a pickup game with a ten-year-old.

Marcus was quick on his feet, and it was easy to see that he had talent.

"You're pretty good," James said after Marcus got around him for a third time.

"Thanks." Marcus bounced the ball from one hand to the other before passing it to James. "I want to try out for the school team next year so I've been practicing."

"It's paying off."

James took a shot. Pain ricocheted up his arm, but the ball made it into the basket.

"You're not so bad, either, for an older guy."

James flexed his fingers before pressing his hand to his heart. "Ouch." He glanced at Erika, who watched them play from a picnic table close to the basketball court.

"You know what I mean." Marcus shot the ball. It bounced off the backboard and into the basket. "My friend Devin is going to try out for the team, too, and sometimes we play two on two with his fathers. They're your age but they can never play a full forty-minute game without getting tired."

James bit back his laughter. "Well, it's not as easy when you're our age."

Marcus stepped up to the foul line. "I guess so. I like playing with them, though. My mother doesn't know anything about basketball and I don't have anyone else to practice with. My dad died before I was born and no siblings." Marcus took a shot. It bounced off the rim.

James chased it down, thinking about what Marcus had just said. The plight of the only child wasn't something that he was familiar with, not with three younger brothers always underfoot, but he was more interested in the comment about Marcus's father. Ronald Overholt died in a car accident almost eleven years ago. The timing was right.

He passed the ball back to Marcus. "I'm sorry about your father. Did he play basketball, too?"

"Um… I don't know," Marcus said distractedly, passing the ball back and forth from hand to hand behind his back.

"Your mom never told you anything about him?"

The moment the words left his mouth, James felt like a jerk. He was pumping a child for information on his late father. If he had any doubt that he wasn't cut out for investigative work, the wave of contempt he felt for himself put it to rest.

Marcus pressed the basketball to his chest and eyed James with suspicion. "Not much. She doesn't like to talk about him."

James could feel Marcus closing off, and the loss felt like a punch to the gut. "Here, can I show you a little trick that will help you with your free throws?"

He had Marcus widen his stance just a bit and showed him how to loosen his wrist more and let it fall forward more naturally as he took the shot. The awkwardness from moments earlier faded away as the ball sailed through the air and into the basket.

"Wow, thanks," Marcus said with a smile that sent a bolt of pride sailing through James's chest.

"Not bad for an old dude, huh?" He gave Marcus's shoulder a pat. "I may not be much of a ballplayer but my brother Brandon was all-state in high school. I paid attention."

"Is he coming to visit you soon?" Marcus's grin was wide.

"Alright, alright. Why don't you practice a bit more while I take my old bones over and talk to your mom."

James walked toward Erika, an unfamiliar feeling rising inside. Marcus was caring, intelligent and quick-witted—a great kid. James hadn't had a lot of contact with kids. Ryan and his wife had just had their first child, and while James knew her three uncles would spoil her as rotten as her parents allowed, she was still an infant.

He sat on the bench next to Erika, pressing his hand against his thigh. All the bouncing and shooting had aggravated his injury. The palm of his hand felt as if it was vibrating.

"Thank you for doing that."

"No problem. He's good and, more importantly, he's a terrific kid."

"He is." She smiled.

"He mentioned his father passed away. I'm sorry."

Erika stiffened. "Thank you." A beat of silence hung between them. "What's wrong with your hand?"

So she'd noticed. He gave his standard answer. "Damaged tendon."

"Is that why you left the military?"

Silence stretched between them for a long moment before he answered. "Yes."

"What happened?"

He thought about evading, shutting down the line of conversation as he normally did whenever anyone but Ryan or one of the other guys he'd served with brought up his time in the military. But he surprised himself when he realized he wanted Erika to know.

"A suicide bomber." The words made his lungs constrict. He beat back the images that threatened to deluge him and forced himself to continue. "A piece of shrapnel tore through my palm. Can't have a marine sniper who can't shoot straight so I took a medical discharge."

There must be something in the water in Carling Lake. In the span of two hours, he'd shared his story with more people than he had in the last six months.

Erika covered his hand with hers. "I'm sorry."

"Thanks, but there are a lot of guys who have it harder than I do." And a lot of guys who didn't make it home. He had no right to complain or wallow.

"That doesn't change your loss," Erika said as if she'd read his mind.

He wasn't so sure she was right, but he didn't want to discuss it, either. "That's part of why I'm in Carling Lake. To take some time and figure out what I want to do with the rest of my life."

Erika's mouth turned up into a smile. "How's it going?"

"So far, not good. I went to the shooting range with the sheriff earlier today. He seems to think I could pass the firearms test to become a sheriff's deputy but I'm not sure law enforcement is for me."

"What is for you?"

He thought about the call from the gallery owner and the dozens of drawings he had in his apartment before pushing the thought away. Becoming a professional artist was an even more fantastical idea than joining the Carling Lake sheriff's department.

"I have no clue," he answered honestly.

"I was in a similar place when I first came to Carling Lake."

He arched an eyebrow. "How so?" He watched

as she wrestled with whatever she was about to say. If she was really Erika Overholt, she'd spent years keeping that secret. He couldn't believe she would just blurt out the truth to a virtual stranger in the park.

"I married Marcus's father when I was twenty-one. My mother had just died, and I was alone. I met my husband, and he seemed like my knight in shining armor. By the time I realized he was anything but, I felt trapped. I got married right out of college. Never had a real profession. My husband was not nice. He made sure I was completely dependent on him. Then he died, and I found out I was pregnant. And that's a whole different level of terror. But eventually Marcus and I landed in Carling Lake, and I don't know, one day at a time I figured things out. I'm sure you will, too."

Erika shook her head, and he got the feeling she was shaking away the painful memories.

His gut twisted with the instinct to protect this woman and her son. And to show the man who was supposed to have protected them, who'd been lucky enough to have had Erika in his bed every night, just what he thought of him.

Which was something he was definitely not supposed to be thinking or feeling. Yet with each passing day, Erika filled more and more of his thoughts. The floral fragrance of her perfume. The kindness in her smile. The way her cheeks flushed when she was irritated or angry.

"We should get going," Erika said, pulling him

from his thoughts. She rose and walked toward the basketball court.

Marcus trotted over to meet her, then looked past her at James. "See ya later, James. Maybe we can play again?"

He waved at the boy. "Anytime." It shocked him to realize just how much he meant it. Wrong or right, he was falling for Erika and her son.

Chapter Ten

"I understand. If your schedule opens up…" Erika heard the dial tone before she ended her statement "…please let me know."

She set her phone down on the table and crossed off the last name on the list of contractors she'd written up when she'd gotten home from the hospital earlier that day. There was no one within a thirty-mile radius who could take on her job immediately.

She glanced out of the kitchen window at James's cabin. Well, almost no one.

On the drive home after her run-in with Ellis, she'd vowed that her B&B would be up and running by the start of the tourist season as planned.

Buying the house and turning it into a B&B had become her dream not long after she'd moved to Carling Lake. It had taken years to earn the money for the down payment on the house and several more to save enough for the renovations that would be needed to turn it into a B&B.

She'd come home and, after throwing together a quick dinner, then getting Marcus started on his homework, redoubled her efforts to find a contractor by expanding her search window.

Her determination had yielded no results. Every business owner in Carling Lake and the surrounding tourist-oriented towns were sprucing up for the tourist season. Any contractor worth their salt, and some who weren't—she knew because in desperation she'd called them, too—had been booked months ago.

She could handle some of the work herself. Two of the guest rooms and a bathroom upstairs needed painting, but the rooms also needed their hardwood floors refinished and she wanted to install a new vanity and toilet in the bathroom. Those were renovations she didn't trust herself to do, at least not well. And she couldn't afford for them not to be done well.

First impressions mattered. She didn't want the B&B to get a reputation for being rundown or shabby. Everything had to be perfect when she opened the doors to her first guests.

And she'd do everything in her power to make it happen, even trusting the very attractive stranger renting the cabin next door.

She glanced out the window a second time, but again just saw the side of the cabin. She had to admit James West looked like he knew his way around a power tool.

She looked out again. *So what's the plan then, Erika?*

"Why do you keep looking out the window?" She turned to find Marcus looking at her quizzically from across the table, where he worked on his homework.

She took a deep breath before answering. "Because I need to go talk to our neighbor. To ask him a favor."

Marcus cocked his head to the side. "So go ask. You always tell me that if I need help, I should just ask and that most people like to help."

She had said that, but she'd been thinking more along the lines of help with algebra and sentence diagrams, not letting a stranger into their lives.

As the years passed in Carling Lake, she'd let her guard down somewhat, befriending Lance and Daisy. But she'd remained on guard, mostly. She could not let Roger Overholt know he had a grandson. There was no way the billionaire philanthropist and businessman would allow them to live in peace. He'd want to have complete control over Marcus, his heir, just like he'd controlled Ronald. And he'd do anything to get it. She wouldn't allow it.

But Marcus didn't know any of that. By the time he'd been born, she'd had her Erika Powell identity in place and had given him her last name. He didn't know he was an Overholt. Didn't know they were essentially hiding from his birth father's family. And she didn't want him to know. She couldn't give him the material things Roger Overholt could, but she'd worked hard to give him a normal childhood free from the fear and terror she'd felt living as an Overholt, and that was priceless.

"You're right," Erika said, standing. "I'm going to

talk to him. I'll just be a minute. You keep working on that algebra." She left the house, crossed the two front yards and knocked on the cabin door before she allowed herself to overanalyze the situation further.

She wasn't inviting James into her and Marcus's lives. She was taking him up on his offer to do work on the house. He'd be working for her, nothing more. If he was still wanted the job, that was. She had been pretty rude when he'd extended the offer. He may not be willing to help her out now.

All these thoughts ran through her brain in the seconds between her knocking and James opening the door.

And then all thought fled. James stood in the doorway in a form-fitting sleeveless T-shirt that clung to his sweaty chest. On his right biceps was a tattoo of an eagle and the letters *USMC*. His dark mesh shorts revealed equally muscled calves and thighs.

"Erika? Everything okay?"

"Yes. Great. I'm…good." She shook her head. *Get it together! He's just a man*. But it had been a while since she'd been with a man. Especially one who looked like the one standing in front of her. No. Scratch that. She'd never been with a man who looked like James West.

James's forehead crinkled with concern. "Erika, you're starting to worry me here. Are you sure you're okay?"

"Does your offer to help with the work on the house still stand?" she blurted out. Her mind had obviously decided to forcibly take the reins from her libido.

"Oh…sure. Yes, of course it still stands." Despite his words, she couldn't help but note the look of surprise on his face.

"If you've changed your mind, I understand. I wasn't very gracious about your offer earlier and I apologize for that."

He smiled, and a ripple of sexual awareness traveled through her. There had been men after Ronald, but it had been a while since her last relationship, and James West was incredibly sexy.

Her pulse kicked into high gear.

"One thing you should know about me," James said, seemingly oblivious to her reaction to him, "is I don't say things I don't mean. I'm ready and willing to help in any way I can."

She felt her shoulders fall and realized how much tension she'd been carrying in them. "Great. Thank you. I know we still need to work out payment but I'm kind of in a time crunch."

He waved a hand, dismissing her statement. "There's no need to pay me. You'd be giving me something to do with myself. How about I get started tomorrow morning?"

She would pay him, but tomorrow was soon enough to fight that battle if need be. "Great. Wonderful. See you tomorrow. If you come over around seven, you can have breakfast with me and Marcus before you get started," Erika said, already walking backward toward her house.

"I'm looking forward to it." His smile grew, and she turned away, physically fighting the urge to run back into her house.

She'd done it. She'd asked for help, and he'd agreed.

Now she just hoped she wouldn't regret it.

Chapter Eleven

"Reed Johnson is a marine. Do you know him?" Marcus pushed his frameless glasses up the bridge of his nose and stared across the table at James expectantly.

"I can't say I do. There are a lot of marines," James answered the latest in the barrage of questions Marcus had asked about the Marine Corps and the military. From all appearances, Marcus and Erika had been up and at 'em for quite some time. The house had smelled of freshly brewed coffee and pancake batter already sizzled on the stove when James arrived promptly at seven o'clock.

Marcus nodded his head knowingly. "Charlie Mulhern is a sailor. That means he's in the Navy."

"I can't say I've met him either I'm afraid." James sipped his coffee, amused and flattered by the young boy's enthusiasm.

Erika headed for the table with a serving plate loaded with pancakes. "There are a lot of people in the military. You can't expect Mr. West to know them all."

He sent Erika a grateful smile. He wasn't used to being around children, especially not ones as inquisitive as Marcus.

He could already tell Erika would be an excellent B&B owner and hostess. She manned the six-burner stove like a professional chef, preparing three different kinds of pancakes—banana-nut, strawberry and a rainbow-sprinkle for him and Marcus to pass judgment on as possible breakfast offerings for future B&B guests. He wasn't sold on strawberry, but the other two definitely earned his stamp of approval.

Marcus ate with gusto, reminding him of how often his father had complained about the massive amounts of food he and his three brothers consumed as teens.

Erika joined them at the table, and they all tucked into breakfast.

Marcus polished off four large pancakes before he spoke again. "Do you like fishing?"

"I haven't done it in a long time but, yes, I do," James answered, bringing his coffee cup to his lips.

"Mom and I are going next Saturday. Do you want to come with us?"

He did. It amazed him, but he was finding that the more time he spent with Erika and Marcus, the more time he wanted to spend with them. A dicey situation, given that he didn't know how Erika would feel about him by next week.

Erika swallowed the bite of pancake in her mouth hurriedly. "I'm sure James has other plans for his weekend. We wouldn't want to impose."

Marcus's face fell.

He hated to disappoint Marcus, but inserting himself into their lives too far risked even greater disappointment later.

"I'm not sure I'll be free next weekend, but can I have a rain check?"

"Sure, whatever," Marcus responded sullenly.

"It's almost time for school. Go finish getting ready. And don't forget to brush your teeth," Erika called after him as he headed through the door at the rear of the kitchen.

"Sorry about that. Let me show you around the house while Marcus is getting ready for school." Erika motioned toward a long hallway to the right of the foyer.

She raised her hands and gestured. "Well, this is the kitchen. As you can see, there's not much to do here. I had it renovated when we moved in four years ago because, well, because we needed to eat." She pointed to the door Marcus had disappeared behind. "Through that door are my and Marcus's bedrooms and a small private sitting room. You don't have to worry about that area."

Erika turned and began walking back toward the entrance hall. With its massive, curved staircase including intricately carved wood railings, it would make quite the impression.

"You probably noticed the large sitting room when you came in. Then there's what used to be the small sitting room. I've turned it into a library for guests who want a little quiet area." She led him down a long hallway and into a room with several four-top round tables. "Here's the dining room where I'll be serving a buffet breakfast."

"The banana-nut pancakes get my vote," James said, stepping into the room after her.

Erika turned, bumping into him and stumbling.

He reached out and steadied her.

"Sorry, I...didn't see you," she said breathlessly. The desire in her eyes kicked his heartbeat up a notch.

Erika stepped back out of his arms, and he fought the need to pull her to him again. "I was just going to say I don't know why I'm showing you all this. The work that needs to be done is on the second floor."

He moved aside and Erika moved past him, out of the room and back toward the front of the house. He let out a deep breath meant to steady his raging libido, and followed her upstairs.

"There's a third floor I hope to open up to guests one day." Erika pointed upward as they reached the second-floor landing. "But for now I just have the rooms on this floor available."

Erika opened the door on the left. They stepped into a sunbathed room with medium-brown wood wainscoting and matching wood framing the windows. "All the bedrooms are pretty much the same. The upper walls need a fresh coat of paint but I don't want to touch the wainscoting or window trim. The floors do need refinishing though."

"And how many rooms are there?" he asked, taking stock of the project. Painting was tedious work but not difficult. Refinishing the floors would be the biggest lift, but he'd helped Ryan refinish the floors in his new house, so he knew the process.

"Four bedrooms and two bathrooms up here." Erika led the way out of the room. She opened another door farther down the hall. "This is the first bathroom. It's dated but everything works so I'm not touching it for now."

James took a quick look around the bathroom and agreed with Erika's assessment. She took him to the door at the end of the hall. "This is the second bathroom."

She opened the door, and he saw right away why she'd been so distressed when Sam Hogan had walked out on her. The bathroom had no vanity or toilet and the light fixture that should have been hanging over the medicine chest sat in the tub.

"It looks worse than it is. The old vanity and toilet were pink with gold flecks. Way too 1960s for the feel I want. Sam was just helping me give the space a more contemporary look. I've ordered the vanity and toilet already but I don't know the first thing about installing them."

"I can help with that." He'd never actually installed a vanity or toilet, but how hard could it be. With the help of the internet, he was sure he could figure it out.

She closed the door and led him back down the front staircase. "You really think you can handle all this?" Erika chewed her bottom lip.

James was suddenly hit with the urge to promise

her anything that would wipe that worried expression off her face.

"Yes. I've refinished floors and anyone can paint walls. I've never installed a vanity or toilet before but I've seen the actors in the commercials do it." His attempt at a joke did nothing to wipe the skepticism from her eyes. "Honestly, I've got this. You said you already ordered the vanity?"

Erika nodded. "From Laureano's hardware store. It should be in any day now."

"Then I'm sure there's someone there who can help me if I get into trouble. I'll be fine."

She watched him for a moment longer, then gave a small smile. "Okay. You're right. I've learned plenty about renovations and the clerk at the hardware store has been very helpful." Her smile widened, and his heart flip-flopped in his chest.

"So I need to drop Marcus off and then I'll be back to help." She led him back to the kitchen, using the rear staircase, and cleared away the remains of breakfast.

He'd been hoping to have time today to search the house for some proof that she really was Erika Overholt. "If you have other things to get done, I'm sure I'll be fine working by myself."

Erika glanced at him over her shoulder. "I won't be much help but I'm free today after I take Marcus to school." She carried an empty plate and cup to the dishwasher.

And she probably wanted to make sure he knew

what he was doing and wasn't going to ruin her chances of getting the B&B open in time. Smart.

He followed her, handing over his dishes.

"I was thinking you could work each day while Marcus goes to school but it's kind of a madhouse around here when he gets home," she said as she rinsed the syrup off his plate before putting it in the dishwasher next to her own. "Getting dinner together and doing homework. I think it would be better for Marcus's studies if there were no renovation distractions. I think we can still get everything done with that work schedule. Don't you?"

"I don't see why not. If we need to, we can always put in longer hours as we near your deadline for submitting the occupancy paperwork."

Marcus appeared in the kitchen doorway. "Mom. I'm ready. Let's go!"

Erika rolled her eyes. "I'm being summoned. Everything we need should be in the basement. Far right corner. The prior owners left an old electric sander. I figured you could use that, but it's too heavy for me to haul up the stairs. Would you mind?"

"Not a problem."

"Great. Back in twenty."

The back door to the house slammed closed as he made his way downstairs. Twenty minutes wasn't a lot of time to search a house of this size, but if there was proof of Erika's real identity in the house, he'd be most likely to find it in the private quarters. Maybe he'd get lucky and be done with this assignment today, after all.

He headed back through the kitchen to the door that Erika indicated led to her private quarters. It opened onto a nice-sized living space with a comfortable looking sectional sofa situated in front of a television. A desk was pushed into one corner of the room; a laptop and a stack of papers sitting on top. He noted several paintings of Carling Lake gracing the sunny yellow walls, clearly not done by a professional but they were very good, nonetheless. Two large windows looked out over the backyard and the trees beyond. A short hallway led to three closed doors. The overall feel of the space was lived in and cozy.

He went to the desk first. It wasn't a very imaginative place to hide anything but then many people weren't all that imaginative when attempting to hide things. The most common hiding places were behind photos, the underside of drawers, behind the toilet or even inside of one, and the oldie but not so goodie under the mattress.

He checked all the usual spots in the living room and bathroom before moving on to the bedroom. Marcus's room was a blue with glow-in-the-dark star and planet stickers pressed onto the ceiling and walls. A pair of Captain America pajamas were strewn across the unmade twin bed. Toys, books and a single shoe sat atop the dresser and a second laptop was on the desk in this room.

He did a quick search of the room, including looking between the mattress and box spring, but he was fairly confident that Erika wouldn't hide anything that could identify her as Erika Overholt in here. It would be far too easy for Marcus to accidentally come across it.

Instinct and experience told him that he'd most likely find proof of Erika's true identity in her bedroom. That was if there was any evidence in the house at all. There was always the chance that she'd rented a safety deposit box at a bank or that there was no proof to be found whatsoever.

Time was dwindling.

He crossed the hall to Erika's bedroom and opened the door. The walls in this room were a soft gray and a gray-and-white rug took up most of the floor. The room was larger than Marcus's but the dark wood king-sized four-poster bed, matching vanity and dresser took up a lot of the extra space. An off-white duvet covered the mattress and a bevy of pillows rested against the headboard. The smell of lilacs lingered in the air, triggering an image of Erika in his mind. He could imagine her here, getting dressed for the day or propped up against the pillows, reading before turning in for the night.

He shook his head, dispelling the distracting images and thoughts and got to work.

As he'd done in the living room, he checked behind the paintings of Carling Lake and the mirror on the vanity before lifting the mattress. Nothing. The single drawer in her night table also revealed nothing of interest.

He wasn't surprised. If Erika Powell really was Erika Overholt, she'd been hiding that fact for a very long time. She wasn't likely to leave evidence of her real identity someplace he'd easily find it. The bedroom had a single narrow walk-in closet on the wall opposite the bed. The folding door was off its track and he fought the urge to put it to rights. Dresses hung next to a row of skirts followed by a handful of blouses. Several pairs of slacks pulled up the rear of the most organized closet he'd ever seen. Jeans and sweaters, all neatly folded, were stacked on the shelf above. Below the hanging clothes was a tidy row of shoes—heels, flats, low-slung booties and knee-length boots. Erika obviously had a thing for shoes.

Going through Erika's closet felt weirdly intimate and guilt stabbed at him as he did. Would she hate him if she found out he'd invaded her space? He couldn't blame her if she did. Just another sign that he was not cut out to be a private investigator. He searched the pockets, the interior of the shoes and behind the stacked clothing, careful to put everything back just as it had been. If there was anything there, Erika had hidden it exceptionally well.

He closed the closet door, making sure to leave it slightly askew as he'd found it.

He was out of time. Erika would be back at any moment and, if he didn't want her to ask questions about what he'd been doing while she was gone, he needed to get that sander upstairs.

He found the sander just where Erika said it would be in the basement. Thankfully, it was a newish lighter-weight model than the huge drum sanders of the past.

He carried it up the two flights of stairs and was only slightly winded when he set it down in the bedroom.

He turned to head back downstairs for the rest of the tools when footsteps sounded below.

He glanced out of the bedroom window. The driveway where she parked her van was still empty.

Whoever was in the house, it wasn't Erika.

His nine-millimeter was locked up in his cabin—he hadn't expected to need it to sand floors. That was a mistake he wouldn't make again.

He snuck down the curved staircase, hoping the creaky wood wouldn't give away his position. Whoever was in the house must have seen Erika drive away and assumed it was empty. An assumption the intruder would come to regret.

In the foyer, James stilled, listening for any sounds. Silence reigned for long enough that he'd just about concluded he'd imagined footsteps when a rustling sound came from the direction of the kitchen.

Definitely not imagined.

He moved into the kitchen, keeping his eyes and ears peeled for any movement or sound. The room was empty. He headed for the door to Erika's private residence. He could hear someone moving around on the other side of the door.

Without a weapon, his best bet was the element of surprise.

James flung the door open, charging into the room, his eyes scanning the space quickly.

And landing on Erika, who stood in front of a desk, steps from the door, a sheath of paper in her hands. She shrank back, her mouth open, ready to scream.

He stopped, just missing barreling into her.

They stared at each other for a moment, and then Erika's face hardened. "What do you think you're doing?"

"I heard footsteps down here and you'd left," he explained quickly. "I thought your would-be burglar might be making a second attempt."

She shook the papers in her hand. "Marcus left his homework. I came back for it."

He held his hands up in surrender. "I'm sorry. I may have over—"

The sound of a thud overhead had him stopping mid-apology. Erika's eyes went to the ceiling, letting him know she'd heard it, too.

"Did Marcus come inside with you?" he asked in a whisper.

She shook her head. "I left him in the car around back."

The sound of footsteps thundering down the front staircase sent him bolting back toward the door. "Lock yourself in the car with Marcus, and don't get out for any reason," he called over his shoulder.

He caught a flash of a man dressed in all black dashing through the front door of the house as he ran through the kitchen for the foyer. He hit the porch at a full sprint in time to see the intruder duck into the woods on the other side of Erika's long driveway.

He didn't bother to chase the guy this time. He

turned back to the house as Erika stepped out onto the porch with a rifle at the ready.

"He got away?" Erika's face was ashen, but she held the rifle in steady hands.

He nodded and climbed the porch steps, his frustration with himself flaring over having lost the intruder for a second time. "Marcus okay?"

"Locked in his room. I figured he'd be safer there than in the car and I wanted to be ready if our visitor circled back." She patted the barrel of the rifle.

"Let's give Marcus the all clear and call Sheriff Webb." He reached to open the screen door.

Erika grabbed his hand to stop him. Warmth spread through him at her touch.

"We can't call Lance."

"Someone is obviously targeting you."

Erika stepped closer. "Listen to me. No one can know about this, do you understand? No one."

Chapter Twelve

"I don't understand. I thought you and the sheriff were friends," James said.

Lance was as close a friend as Erika had in Carling Lake, but he didn't—couldn't—know everything about her. The current string of events had the potential to force Lance to look more deeply into her background than she was comfortable with.

"We are. And Lance would do everything he could to find the guy. But I can't afford to have people think my B&B is unsafe."

"There might be more at stake than the B&B's reputation. Assuming this is the same person who tried to break in the night you were in the hospital, they seem determined to keep trying until they get whatever it is they are after."

She could see the wisdom in what James was saying, but she needed time to think. There was a slim chance the events of the last two days meant Roger Overholt had discovered she'd given birth to his grandson, but she suspected the source of her recent troubles might lie closer to home.

"I don't think so."

James sent her a penetrating look. "Is there something you're not telling me?"

If he only knew. But he couldn't know, not if she wanted to ensure she and Marcus would continue to be safe. She had to keep reminding herself. She couldn't even be sure the recent incidents had anything to do with who she'd been.

She set the shotgun across the table on the porch. "I don't have any evidence but I think Ellis Hanes might be behind the break-ins."

"The guy who stole your contractor from you."

"Yes."

James looked as if he were considering it. "I'm not discounting the possibility that Hanes is trying to sabotage your B&B. Corporate espionage isn't exactly new, but your theory wouldn't explain the first attempted break-in. That happened before your contractor walked off the job."

"Ellis still could have sent him."

"Okay, let's say this Hanes guy is behind the break-ins and the bridge. That's all the more reason to report this to the sheriff's department."

"We didn't even get a good look at the man. Lance will come out and take our statements and nothing will come of it except that people will hear about another incident—" she used air quotes "—at my B&B."

"Erika—"

"Just stop, okay. You don't get it. Calling Lance would be a waste of time. Ellis Hanes and his family are revered in this town. Nobody will take my side against his even if they do believe me. I'm on my own here," she said, her voice breaking as the raw truth of that statement hit her. She lowered her head, fighting the tears and wariness. The weight of not only the last several days but the last ten years, years spent concerned that Roger Overholt would show up out of the blue or that someone would discover her real identity.

James stepped forward, reached down and hooked her chin with his forefinger, lifting it until her eyes met his. "You're not on your own. You have me."

His words rumbled through her. The same physical awareness she'd felt when he'd given her a ride home from the hospital and given him a tour of the B&B earlier in the day flooded her body.

He moved his hands to her upper arms, rubbing them softly.

She stepped closer, stepping into his embrace when his arms encircled her waist. His hard muscled body pressed against her softer form.

James's eyes never left hers, and the look on his face was intense and intoxicating, beckoning her to lean in and taste his full lips. The butterflies in her stomach kicked up another notch. He lowered his head slowly, giving her a chance to back away.

She knew it was a bad idea, but she wanted him to kiss her more than she had wanted anything in a very long time.

Before she could talk herself out of it, she raised her head and met his kiss.

He caressed her lips with a firm, slightly demanding kiss that sent a surge of excitement through her. She deepened the kiss, felt his surprise at her aggressiveness before he let her take the lead.

She might have completely lost herself in his embrace, but the sounds from inside the house yanked her back into reality.

She placed a hand on his chest and stepped back. "We can't. Marcus might see and you're only here for a short time."

Disappointment spread across his face, but was quickly replaced by acceptance. "I understand."

"I just think it's better if we keep things…" *Casual* wasn't the right word. That implied that she was open to more kissing, maybe even more than kissing. Was she? She let her gaze travel over the man in front of her. No, she wasn't a casual fling kind of woman. And she had a son to think about. "Professional. It's best that we keep things friendly, but professional."

"Friendly but professional," James said the words as if they were foreign to him. And the intensity of his stare hadn't eased since she'd broken off the kiss.

"Yes."

"If that's what you want."

"I should get Marcus to school." She grabbed the rifle from the table and turned to go into the house.

"I guess I should get back to work."

She felt his solid presence as he fell into step behind her.

Friendly but professional. It wasn't what she wanted, but it was what was best.

She had to keep telling herself that. And maybe, eventually, she'd even believe it.

Chapter Thirteen

Erika had kept her distance from James in the two days since their smoldering kiss. She'd held up her part of their deal and continued to make breakfast, but she'd allowed Marcus to dominate the conversation with his unceasing questions about the military and what it was like to live in New York City.

She'd liked the kiss a lot. It had awakened feelings she hadn't even thought about in a decade. Despite her intention to keep James at arm's length, she found herself thinking about him often. There was something in the way he looked at her. As if she were the most interesting woman in the world and he couldn't take his eyes off her. But there were too many complications to pursue those feelings. James would go back to his life eventually and it wouldn't be fair to him or Marcus to pull him too close when whatever they could have would be based on lies.

She'd hoped to have time to help with the renovation, but she'd mostly kept to the private residence space she and Marcus shared, focusing on her work for the *Weekly*.

That was where she now sat, at the small desk she'd crammed into a corner of the living room, putting the finishing touches on a story about Moulton's new flavor to kick off the tourist season, she'd been tapping every resource she had in an effort to get to the bottom of the mystery of the missing grant money. Unfortunately, she hadn't turned up anything except a renewed resolve for answers. Which was why she had decided that she needed to pay another visit to the treasurer's office.

Susan Garraus had been less than helpful when Erika had brought the first letter granting Carling Lake the money to the town treasurer's attention. She'd claimed to have heard nothing about it at all, but something about her denials hadn't rung completely true to Erika's ears. But without any proof that Susan wasn't being honest, there'd been nothing Erika could do.

Maybe now, with this apparent demand letter from the government, Susan would be more forthcoming.

Erika glanced at her watch. It was 2:12 p.m. The middle school let out at four o'clock. That left plenty of time to talk to Susan before she had to pick up Marcus. She grabbed her purse, pulled the door open and stepped into the kitchen. She stopped short when she caught sight of James at the island, a fresh pot of coffee in the machine.

"There's enough for two if you want a cup," he said before taking a sip from the mug in his hands.

"Thanks. I'm good. I was on my way out, actually."

"Where are you headed?"

"I need to pop into the town treasurer's office to check into something for a story I'm working on. I shouldn't be too long."

"I'll go with you." James took a big gulp from the mug, then set it in the sink.

"No. I don't think that is a good idea." She took a step toward the back door.

"The hardware store called. The vanity is in. I can pick it up while you do whatever you need to do. It doesn't make sense for us to drive separate cars."

His statement was logical, but she felt like being in the car with him would be too awkward.

"We should talk about the kiss. It obviously made you uncomfortable—"

"No, we shouldn't and it didn't." Her gaze slid from his.

"Really? Because you've barely spoken to me or looked at me in the last two days and you don't even want to take a five-minute ride into town with me."

"Fine. You're right. You can come with me to pick up the vanity."

She turned her back to him and went to the van. He slid into the passenger seat as she started the car.

They rode in silence, his statement about their kiss replaying on a loop through her mind until she pulled into a parking space outside of city hall.

She put the van in park, cut the engine and turned in her seat to face James. "The kiss... Our kiss. It didn't make me uncomfortable. At least not the way you're probably thinking. It's just… I haven't been kissed like that in a very long time. It was nice." That was the understatement of the decade. "Very nice, but it can't happen again. I just don't have room in my life for…complications. I have Marcus to consider and the B&B renovation. You're not going to be in town that long, and there's this person breaking into my house—" She felt herself babbling.

"I get it. I do," James interrupted. "Look, I get that things are complicated right now." He hesitated and for a moment his face darkened and she got the sense he was about to share a secret with her. But then his expression softened. "I don't want to make things harder for you but I can't deny there's something between us."

"James—"

"Wait, hear me out. I told you that I'm in Carling Lake to figure out what comes next in my life. That means taking stock and being honest with myself and what I want. You and I are bound to be…complicated." The shadow passed over his face again before clearing just as quickly. He reached across the console for her hand. "But that doesn't mean it's not worth a shot."

She felt herself weakening.

"I can't talk about this right now. I need to get to the treasurer's office." Erika exited the van. James did the same and fell into step beside her. She stopped and turned to him. "The hardware store is that way." She pointed over her shoulder.

"I know. I figured I'd go with you and then we could both walk over to get the vanity."

"Why? I mean I can handle this on my own."

"I'm sure you can, but I've always wanted to see a journalist in action."

"James—"

The look on his face brooked no nonsense. "We're wasting time."

The tension in Erika's body only heightened once she was inside the Carling Lake treasurer's office.

Carling Lake town treasurer, Susan Garraus, stood at the counter in the front office. Her eyes flicked to James and a slow coquettish smile slid across her face.

A flicker of jealousy rose in Erika's chest, watching Susan check out James. Susan was about ten years older than Erika's thirty-seven, but she was still an attractive woman. Shiny brown hair fell in waves to her shoulders and while her designer glasses definitely contributed to a librarian-ish aura, the look veered more toward sexy librarian than frumpy librarian.

Susan's gaze turned to Erika and her expression hardened, her lips puckering as if she'd just bitten into something extremely sour.

"Hi, Susan. I'm hoping you can help me out. You might recall our conversation a few weeks ago about an award of a grant by the federal—"

"I recall," Susan cut her off. "And as I told you then, there is no grant."

Erika kept her smile. "I received another letter."

She pulled a copy of the attachments from both the emails from her purse and laid them on the desk facing Susan. "This one looks like a demand from the government asking Carling Lake to show that the grant money is being used as specified in its application. Carling Lake may not have applied for the grant or received any money, but it sure seems like the federal government thinks it did. I'm sure you can see how that's a problem that the citizens of Carling Lake deserve to know how their elected officials are handling it." She reached back into her purse and pulled out a small notebook.

These days most reporters recorded their interviews using their phones but New York required all parties to a conversation to consent to a recording. Consent Erika doubted Susan would give her. Interviewees were more forthcoming when she used pen and paper, anyway. There was something about the old-school method that people found less intimidating.

Susan's eyes narrowed to slits. "It's not a problem because there is no grant. I don't know who's sending you these letters or what they are filling your head with but it's all fake."

"The letters are addressed to this office." Erika pointed to the salutation. "Are you saying you've never seen them before?"

"I'm telling you, I know nothing. About. A grant."

Susan's persistent denials only intensified the feeling in Erika's gut that she was lying. She glanced over at James, who hadn't said a word since they'd entered, but whose face reflected disbelief as well. "Have you spoken to anyone in the federal government to find out what's going on?"

"I don't have to answer that," Susan sneered.

"So the treasurer's office is not at all concerned that it might be on the hook for three hundred thousand dollars no one seems to know anything about?"

Susan's face turned red, but she simply stared across the counter at Erika.

"Is that a no comment from the treasurer's office, then?"

Susan pursed her mouth and turned away, disappearing into a rear office without another word.

"That went well," James said as he followed her from the office.

"About as well as every conversation I've had with Susan over the last couple of weeks has gone. The thing is I'm sure she knows something about this grant money." They exited the building and turned toward the hardware store.

"I have to agree with you there," James said. "She was definitely nervous about something. What is the story with the grant?"

She quickly filled him in. "I've tapped into every source I have. My boss even has a few calls out to his own sources but so far, nothing."

"I know a couple of vets who work for the feds now. I can't promise anything but I can see if either of them knows anyone who works for the office that distributed the grant."

James's offer was another chink in her armor. "That would be amazing. Thank you."

She was lost in thought as they piled back into the van and headed to pick up the bathroom vanity at the hardware store. That James was going out of his way to help her even though they'd just met touched her. It had been a long time since she'd had someone step up for her. Of course, there were Lance and Daisy but it was different with James.

Different because your feelings for him are much more than friendly. Okay, she was willing to admit it to herself. She was attracted to James West. What did it matter? Feelings or no feelings, she wasn't wrong about not needing additional complications in her life at the moment. Between starting a new business, the attacks on the B&B, her work for the paper and raising Marcus on her own, she had more than enough to keep her busy. And once James figured out his next steps, he'd leave Carling Lake, and her and Marcus, behind.

She snuck a sidelong glance at him as she drove. The most logical decision was to keep things professional. Even if that left her just the tiniest bit crestfallen.

Chapter Fourteen

"It's gorgeous. I love it. Thank you so much, Taria."
Erika threw her arms around Taria Sanders, part-
time clerk at Laureano's hardware and full-time
waitress at Mahoney's Grill. The other woman stiffened, and after giving Erika's back a perfunctory pat,
stepped out of the embrace quickly.

"Sorry."

"No problem." Taria waived the apology away but
the expression on her face left no doubt that the hug
had made her uncomfortable.

Taria had largely kept to herself since she'd come
to town several months earlier. Erika couldn't say she
knew the woman well but she'd been a tremendous
help when it had come to tracking down the semi-
circular light cherrywood antique vanity Erika had
fallen in love with when she'd seen it in an architec-
tural magazine. Erika doubted very much seventy-
two-year-old Vincent Laureano, owner of Laureano's
hardware, would have searched through the dozens
of web pages Taria had to find the manufacturer.

"You paid in advance so you're all set. Let me just go find someone to help you get this into your car."

"That's what I'm here for." James smiled.

Taria blinked. "Okay, well I'll just wrap it back up and push this to the back door. You can load from there."

The vanity was already on a pushcart but Erika had had Taria remove the foam padding wrapped around it so she could inspect it before she officially took possession.

"Actually, I wanted to show you something if you have time," James said, pulling both women's gazes to him.

"Sure." Erika followed him to the rear of the store where a selection of tiles for the floor, shower and kitchen hung on the wall and populated the shelves.

"I took a look at the bathroom where you want the vanity installed. The bathtub and the tile around it look pretty good but you could stand to upgrade the flooring. Right now, it's a vinyl tile, in okay shape. But I was thinking if you're going through all the trouble of installing a new vanity and toilet, you may as well upgrade the floors."

Erika ran her hands over the black-and-white hexagonal shaped tile she'd had her eye on for a while. She'd had Sam price out the cost of changing the floors when he'd given her an estimate for doing the renovations but she'd only had the budget for necessary repairs—the vanity and toilet weren't just old, they leaked, which ate into her profits. The bathroom floor, as James noted, was okay.

She shook her head. "I got an estimate for changing the floors. I don't have the budget."

"Did your estimate account for free labor and the store's discount on flooring?" He pointed to the sign declaring all flooring ten percent off.

Sam's estimate had definitely included a charge for labor and a ten-percent discount was enticing. She did a rough calculation in her head. It would put her over her budget for the bathroom but only a little.

She cocked her head and looked at James. "Why would you add another reno project to the work we agreed you'd do for free?"

"I have the time and I want to help. That's all there is to it."

She very much doubted that. The price for his time and labor they'd finally agreed upon was already low but she'd been desperate and he'd refused to take any more. It had probably been the first and only time in history where a contractor negotiated the fee down while the customer was negotiating up.

"Okay but only if I pay you the ten percent I'm saving on the tiles. It's fair and it's the only way I'll agree," she added, stopping his protest before it got started.

"It's a deal." He stretched his arm out. She slid her hand in his, sending sparks racing through her body. Her heart thundered in her chest and she found herself involuntarily closing the space between them.

She couldn't take her eyes off his, which she might have felt self-conscious about if his eyes hadn't also been locked on her gaze, the desire she saw in them warming her from head to toe.

"The vanity is on the loading… Oh, sorry. Didn't mean to interrupt anything." Taria's light brown skin flushed and she turned, hurrying back the way she'd come.

Erika took a large step backward, feeling the heat of embarrassment rising in her face. The last thing she needed was rumors about her and James making out in Laureano's hardware spreading through town.

For his part, James didn't look the least bit embarrassed about almost being caught kissing her in public. He stuck his hands in his pocket and leaned forward, eliminating much of the distance she'd put between them.

A devilish grin, one she found both mildly irritating in its glee and incredibly hot, twisted his lips. "You know that complication you don't have time for right now? I think you might need to make time because whatever this is, it's not going away."

Chapter Fifteen

Taria rang up the tiles and items that were needed to lay them while James maneuvered all the purchases into the back of the van in a way that left enough room for Marcus. Feeling like she was back in high school, Erika had started to explain that nothing had happened between her and James in the tile aisle but Taria had shut down the conversation, saying she wasn't in the habit of sharing other people's business and she didn't have anyone to share it with even if she'd wanted to. That last comment had left her feeling bad for the woman. Taria was probably lonely, having moved to town relatively recently.

Erika made a mental note to invite Taria over for dinner as soon as the renovations were completed, then met James at the van. They pulled into the school parking lot just as the bell rang, signaling the end of the day. The ride home was filled with Marcus regaling them with stories about his day.

She backed the van into the driveway beside the house so the trunk was closest to the door. It would make it easier to move the vanity and tiles from the back into the house.

Marcus got out on the passenger side behind James, explaining in precise detail exactly how he'd made the winning shot in the pickup basketball game he and his buddies played at recess that day.

A flash burst from the trees across from Erika's house, alerting James before his brain actually registered the sound of the gunshot.

He grabbed Marcus's arm and shoved him toward the back of the van, putting the vehicle between them and the shooter.

"Marcus!" Erika yelled.

Without a pause, he drew his gun from the holster at his side. The nerves in his palm pinched as he wrapped his hand around the gun's grip. "Get around to the back of the van and keep your head down," James yelled.

Erika rounded the van on the driver's side and immediately wrapped her body around Marcus in a protective huddle.

A second shot shattered one of the front windows on the house.

James shook his head. "We need to get inside. We're too exposed out here."

Their shooter had gone quiet. It had been nearly half a minute since the second shot, but that wasn't necessarily good news. Although he hadn't seen the shooter, he had a pretty good idea of the approximate area in the trees where the shots had come from. The shooter didn't have a clear line of sight anymore. But that could change quickly. Whoever was shooting at them could be at this very moment moving to get a better angle.

But would he be able to hit his target if it came to that? Just the weight of the gun had set the nerves in his hand to trembling. He had no choice but to try. They were too exposed where they were.

James cut a look at Erika over the top of Marcus's head. "When I tell you to go, run for the front door as fast as you can and stay away from the windows. And Erika as soon as you're safe call Lance."

He hadn't bought for a minute that her hesitancy to call Lance after the break-in had been a way to protect the new B&B's reputation. But someone taking shots at them, that was an escalation that demanded help from the proper authorities.

Erika seemed to agree. She nodded before her eyes fell to his hand, and he knew she'd seen them trembling. "Are you sure—"

"We can't stay here. You know how to use that rifle you were holding the other day. When you get inside, grab it."

She gave another nod.

James peered around the front of the van, looking for any movement in the area the shots had come from. He stepped out from behind the car, firing off several rounds toward the trees and yelling, "Go, go, go!"

Erika and Marcus's footsteps pounded up the porch steps as he got off three more shots, covering them as they made their way into the house.

There was no return fire.

He moved as quickly as he could into the house, slamming the door behind him and turning the deadbolt into place.

Erika and Marcus sat on the kitchen floor between the island and the stove. She had the rifle in one hand and her cell phone in the other.

"Lance is on his way." She held up the phone, and he heard the sheriff's confirmation come from the other end of the open line.

James crouched down, taking the phone from Erika's hand. "I think our shooter is gone, but be careful coming in."

James ended the call.

"Are you sure the bad guy isn't here anymore?" Marcus's voice cracked and tears streaked his cheeks.

James wasn't sure he'd ever felt such an intense rush of anger, but he wrangled it under control for Marcus's sake.

"I don't know, buddy, but don't worry. As long as I'm here, no one is going to hurt you or your mom."

SOMEONE HAD SHOT at them.

The thought terrified Erika. She didn't doubt for a moment that Roger would have her killed if that's what it took to get guardianship of Marcus. She wouldn't let that happen. She'd never allow Marcus to become like his father and grandfather.

Which meant she'd have to run again.

It would be harder this time. She'd have to figure out what to tell Marcus. He wasn't a baby. He'd demand answers, and he deserved them. And he wouldn't be the only person looking for answers. She'd built a life in Carling Lake she couldn't have imagined ten years ago when she'd fled Los Angeles—her job, Lance and Daisy. Maybe most surprisingly, she'd started imagining a future—running the B&B and, recently, picturing what it would be like to open herself up more, to consider the possibility that she didn't have to be alone.

She shot a glance across the room at James. He and Lance spoke in hushed voices in front of the old fireplace, which she had visions of firing up during the cold winter months. As if he could feel her eyes on him, James's gaze tracked to hers and held for a long moment.

Once Lance and his deputies had arrived, they'd moved from the kitchen to the library, where they could all be more comfortable.

She sat on the overstuffed green velvet couch, Marcus tucked into her side. He'd been reluctant to take more than three steps away from her, even after Lance's arrival, which was fine with her. Even though she knew they were no longer in immediate danger, her heart was still struggling to catch up.

Still, something didn't feel right about Roger being behind the shooting. Not that she'd put it past Roger to target her. But Marcus? She couldn't see Roger taking the chance that Marcus would get hurt.

Deputy Bridges escorted Daisy into the library.

"I came as soon as I heard. Are you okay?" Daisy sat down beside Erika and threw an arm around her shoulder in a one-armed hug. The action jostled Marcus awake, who'd been dozing on the other side of Erika with his head on her shoulder.

"We're all a bit shaken up but unharmed," Erika answered, leaning into her friend's side.

Daisy chattered on about how the news that someone had taken a shot at Erika was making its way around town, but the only news Erika was interested in at the moment was whatever Deputy Bridges was saying to Lance and James. She couldn't hear them from where she was sitting on the other side of the room but, from the pinched look on all three men's faces, it wasn't good. The three men crossed the library.

"Hey, Marcus, you think I can talk to your mom alone for a minute?" Lance said.

The sleepy haze fell from Marcus's face, replaced by a steely resolve. In answer to Lance's question, he scooted closer to Erika.

She suspected that Marcus's bravado wasn't totally about protecting her. "It's okay, Marcus. Why don't you show Deputy Bridges that new video game you and Devin can't stop playing?" Hopefully, having Deputy Bridges with him would alleviate some of the fear she knew he was feeling.

"Yeah, come give me some tips so I have a fighting chance when I play against you and Devin from home." Deputy Bridges shot Marcus a reassuring smile.

"Go on. It's okay," Erika said.

Marcus reluctantly rose from the sofa and trudged from the room with Deputy Bridges at his back.

Lance sat on the edge of the armchair across from the couch. James remained standing.

"My deputies combed the area, but unfortunately, we weren't able to find the shooter," Lance began.

Although she'd expected as much, she couldn't help feeling a rush of disappointment. If they could get their hands on the shooter, they might have a chance of nailing down who was behind the various attacks that had been taking place.

"What does that mean? What can we do?" Erika asked.

"Well, the good news is we found shell casings. I'll send them to the state crime lab and forensics will go over them with a fine-tooth comb."

"Okay, what aren't you telling me? I've known you long enough to know when you're keeping something from me." She looked over at James. "What is it?"

James held her gaze. "The three of us were sitting ducks when we pulled up to the house but all the shots were aimed at your side of the car."

Daisy reached for Erika's hand and squeezed. "I don't understand. What does that mean?"

Lance's gaze moved between Erika and Daisy. "We think someone was shooting at you."

The import of Lance's words struck like a fist to the chest. Erika shuddered out a breath. "Someone tried to kill me."

"It's possible," Lance answered.

"The question is who would want to scare you and why?" James said.

"Ellis." Three pairs of eyes locked onto a visibly angry Daisy.

"Daisy—" Erika started.

"Ellis Hanes?" Lance interrupted. "I'd heard he isn't too happy about you opening a B&B. Has he done anything beyond snipe and complain?"

"Not really," Erika said.

"Yes," Daisy said simultaneously.

"He bought off Erika's contractor in a bid to make sure she didn't complete the B&B renovations," James offered.

"And he threatened Erika as she came out of Laureano's hardware store a few days ago. Essentially said she'd better drop the idea of opening a competing B&B or else," Daisy added.

Lance flew out of the armchair. "Why didn't you tell me this before?"

"Because Daisy is exaggerating." Erika shot her friend an angry look. "Ellis did not threaten me. He's not happy I'm opening the B&B, but you can't really believe he'd go this far. I mean my B&B is small potatoes, tiny potatoes, compared to the Carling Lake B&B and his hotel."

"If he didn't see you as a potential threat, he wouldn't have confronted you at all," Daisy pointed out.

It was a sound argument, but still a long way off from proving Ellis had taken those shots.

James's brow furrowed. "Seems like an extreme action to take under the circumstances."

"Ellis mentioned word getting out that your B&B was unsafe," Daisy added pointedly. Her eyes widened. "And that was right after you fell from the bridge. I bet Ellis is responsible for that, too."

Lance held up a hand. "Hang on. I got the lab results back on the rope from the bridge. It was inconclusive so we don't know whether the bridge was deliberately tampered with or if it was just an accident."

Daisy guffawed dramatically. "Come on, Lance. The bridge gives out, someone tries to set fire to the B&B and then Ellis just happens to threaten to spread the rumor that Erika's property is unsafe. That's like three too many coincidences to be coincidences in my book."

"Hanes and I exchanged words earlier this afternoon before the shooting," James interjected. "I came upon him trying to intimidate Erika and while she was holding her own—"

"Of course she was," Daisy huffed.

"—Hanes was not pleased with my butting in," James finished.

Lance's brows knitted. "Not pleased enough that he'd try something like this?"

James shrugged. "You know bullies. They can be volatile when you stand up to them. Especially if they feel threatened. From what I understand, Hanes fancies himself somebody in this town. No telling what he might do when that status is threatened."

The speculation was getting out of hand. Erika couldn't argue with the logic, but Daisy, Lance and James didn't have all the facts. Maybe it was time they did.

"I'm going to have a talk with Ellis." Lance turned to leave.

"Wait, Lance—" Erika said.

"I know you don't think Ellis would be involved in something like this, but this is my job. You and Ellis had a confrontation recently, and he does have a motive to want to paint your property as unsafe, maybe even potentially hurt you. Considering everything that's going on, it's just sound police work to speak with him."

"That's just it. Ellis isn't the only person who could be behind everything that's been happening. He's not even the one with the most motive," Erika says.

Confusion swept over Lance's and Daisy's faces, but James's expression was neutral, almost as if he expected what she'd say next. But he couldn't, could he?

"What do you mean," Lance asked.

"I'm not... My real name is not Erika Powell. It's Erika Overholt. I was married to Ronald Overholt. Marcus is his son."

"Ronald Overholt, the son of the billionaire conglomerate owner Roger Overholt?" Lance said, stunned.

Erika nodded. "Yes. Roger is not the man everyone thinks he is. Ronald wasn't, either, for that matter. After Ronald's death, Roger threw me out—out of my house and out of the family."

Lance's face scrunched up like he was thinking hard about something. "I know the Overholt conglomerate owns a piece of every major industry in the world it seems like."

Erika nodded again. "Roger stays out of the limelight. He thinks celebrities are low-class, but he's one of the richest men in the country, maybe the world now. Ronald is Roger's oldest son. Nearly eleven years ago, he was killed in a single car accident. We were in the car together, but I only suffered minor injuries. I had my seat belt on. Ronald was drunk out of his mind and I shouldn't have gotten into the car with him. Shouldn't have let him drive. But I'd learned early in our marriage there were severe consequences to defying Ronald."

Erika's body tensed with residual anger toward Ronald even as her stomach knotted with anxiety, remembering how small and insignificant she'd felt during the years she'd been Erika Overholt.

Quiet stretched across the room.

"Why didn't you ever say anything? Say…something?" Lance asked, shocked.

Erika could see the hurt in her friend's eyes and regret at having put it there flooding through her. "I couldn't take the chance of telling anyone."

"Wait a minute," Daisy interrupted. "How could Roger Overholt throw you out of your house?" Daisy asked, perplexed. "I mean, I know the man is powerful, but it's your house."

Erika pushed to her feet and paced in front of the sofa. A release for some of the nervous energy coursing through her body. "That's just it. I didn't know it, but it wasn't our house. Everything was in Roger's name—the house, the cars, the bank accounts. Everything. I didn't know... I was a very different woman back then. I started dating Ronald not long after my mother died. I was alone and isolated, and I didn't see just how controlling Ronald was. In the first two years of our marriage, he chipped away at my confidence and self-worth until I didn't recognize myself. I didn't have any family, and I knew Ronald wouldn't let me leave, anyway. It would shatter his perfect appearance, and appearances were everything to Ronald. And Roger. Not that I could ever be perfect enough. They both always found fault with the way I dressed, looked, sat, ate—with *me*."

"Emotional abuse is just as destructive as physical abuse but all too frequently ignored or dismissed," James offered.

Erika shifted her gaze to his and was relieved to find understanding there.

"That's what I did, dismissed it. I told myself it wasn't abuse because Ronald never hit me."

"It is abuse, though," Daisy said while rubbing soothing circles along Erika's back.

"I know that now. If I'd been older, had more life experience, I might have questioned how Stepford-wifey Roger's wife, Dianna, was. Or how odd it was that Roger and Dianna's daughter had fled the moment she was old enough."

Lance frowned. "The Overholt family is pretty well-known. I don't remember a daughter."

"That's because Roger disowned her years ago. Before I even knew Ronald. Evangeline. Apparently, she wouldn't allow Roger to control her life. I only know about her because Ronald got drunk enough one night to mention her and told me a bit about her before he passed out. I remember being jealous that she had the spine to stand up to Roger. Sometimes I think Ronald was, too."

"There's something I don't understand, though," James said with a questioning look in his eye. "If Roger threw you out of the family, why all the subterfuge? I get not wanting to keep the Overholt name but it seems like there's more to this story you haven't told us about yet."

"There is. The most important part really." Erika sighed. "I told you perfection was important to the Overholts, but it wasn't the most important thing. The most important thing was blood, as in Roger Overholt's descendants."

The confused look didn't leave James's face.

"I don't understand," Lance said.

"Roger treated everyone in the family as if they were an extension of him. It was why everyone had to be beyond reproach, unattainably perfect. Roger groomed his sons in his image and, as long as he held the purse strings, they'd do whatever he told them to do. The night of the accident after the doctor delivered the news that Ronald hadn't made it, the doctors told me I was pregnant. I was still trying to process everything when Roger cast me out. I knew I could fight him and probably get something, a nice settlement to keep the Overholt name from being besmirched in the LA tabloids at least, but I also knew the cost of that settlement would be Marcus's life. If Roger knew he had a grandchild, especially a grand*son*, he'd do everything in his power to get and keep Marcus under his thumb. There was no way I was going to let that man anywhere near my son, so I left. Changed my name. Disappeared completely."

"But now you think it's possible Roger Overholt has learned about Marcus and he's behind the shooting today." Lance put her fears into words.

Erika swallowed hard. "Yes. I...don't know who else would come after me like this."

"It's not Roger Overholt," James said, drawing every pair of eyes to him. "Roger Overholt is dead."

Chapter Sixteen

Erika fell back onto the couch, her arms wrapped protectively around her midsection. "How do you…" Erika murmured, suspicion clouding her eyes.

"He's right," Lance interjected, looking up from his phone. "There are a few articles online but I guess, like you said Erika, he wasn't a celebrity so Overholt's death didn't get widespread notice."

James kept his eyes on Erika. Despite Lance's perfectly reasonable assumption that he'd learned about Roger Overholt's demise through the news, James could see that Erika rightly suspected otherwise.

He had what he'd come to Carling Lake for, and he hadn't even had to break any laws. Erika had admitted she was really Erika Overholt. He didn't have documentary proof, but she could hardly deny it after admitting as much in front of Lance and Daisy. He could report back to Ryan, let Erika, Lance and everyone else in town keep on believing that he was just a recently discharged marine figuring out his next steps and fade away.

But he looked into Erika's eyes and knew he couldn't do it.

She deserved to know the truth, even if it meant she'd hate him.

"That's not why I know about Overholt's death." The air in the library stilled. "I know because I'm working for his estate. I work for West Security and Investigations, my family's firm, actually. We were hired by Roger Overholt's executors to find Erika and Marcus."

He kept watching Erika and saw all the blood drain from her face. He felt like he'd been punched in the gut.

"He knew about Marcus. How?" Erika's words were barely a whisper.

"Yes, he knew. How I can't answer but the will directs that all heirs be notified of their bequests at the same time and in the same place, so we were hired to find you. Presumably, you and Marcus have been bequeathed something in the will."

"I don't want it," Erika said quietly. Daisy had rubbed Erika's back again, but Erika shook her off and straightened. "I don't want it." Her voice came stronger now. "I don't want anything from that man. From that family."

"West was only hired to find you and confirm you and your son are Erika and Marcus Overholt. The lawyers will contact you about what's in the will."

Erika sprung from the couch and stalked across the room to stand directly in front of him. "After ev-

erything I just told you about Roger and his family,
you're going to tell them you know where we are?"

He wanted to tell her he wouldn't, that West would
tear up the contract with the estate and return all the
money, but that wasn't his call to make. He'd been
sent here to do a job.

He reached for her, but she stepped away.

"Don't touch me." Her voice shook with rage. "I
can't believe you would do this. I trusted you." She
turned and stormed from the room. Daisy shot him a
disgusted look before hurrying from the room after
Erika.

James started to follow, but Lance stepped in his
way.

"Not so fast." Lance's jaw flexed with anger.
"She's too angry to hear anything you have to say
right now and I have questions."

James felt the muscles in his own jaw tighten with
frustration, but he knew Lance was right. Erika was
furious, as she had a right to be, and he'd do better
to let her cool down some before he tried to explain
himself.

"How much did you know about all that stuff
Erika just told us?"

"None of it," he practically growled. "West was
hired by the estate. Obviously, we knew Overholt
was the billionaire owner of the largest private conglomerate in the US but from our point of view, this
was a simple assignment to confirm an individual's
identity."

Lance's chin rose. "Yet, you've been here for over

a week now. How come you haven't already confirmed who Erika is and gotten out of here?"

James sighed. "Because I'm a horrible PI. Technically, I'm not even a PI. I'm just working for the family company while I get my life sorted. I never lied. I just didn't tell the whole truth."

Lance scoffed. "A distinction without a difference if I've ever heard one."

James couldn't argue with the statement, so he didn't.

"Look, if West had sent anyone else up here, they'd have just broken into the B&B and searched until they found some proof that Erika and Marcus Powell were really Erika and Marcus Overholt. I couldn't do that. That's why I'm still here because I—" He stopped short of completing his sentence.

"Because you care about her." It was Lance's turn to sigh.

There was no sense in denying it, not that he wanted to. "Erika and Marcus. I care about both of them."

"So you're sticking around, then? Because I don't think Roger Overholt has risen from the dead to take potshots at Erika."

"Me, either. Erika is angry right now, but I don't know if I buy that the attacks on her and the house are tied to the Overholts."

"So what do you think is going on?" Lance's voice rose a decibel and he slapped the side of his thigh in aggravation.

"I have no idea," James said, feeling his frustration level rising.

"You didn't answer my earlier question. Are you planning to stay now that the cat is out of the bag?"

James nodded. "Yes." Because even though Erika was furious about his deception, he had no intention of leaving her and Marcus until they got to the bottom of whatever was going on and he knew they were safe. He might not even leave then, if he could convince her to trust him again. But that was not a thought he was willing to share with Lance. "I have a question for you. Why aren't you trying to run me out of town on a rail?"

Lance held up his index finger. "I need you. I can't be here with Erika and Marcus all the time. You, however, can."

James barked out a laugh. "Are you kidding me? Erika wants nothing to do with me. The only reason she hasn't kicked me out of this house is because she's so angry she hasn't thought about it. Yet."

"Well then, you'd better do whatever you have to do to convince her that keeping you around is her safest option before she gets around to kicking you to the curb." Lance stepped closer and lowered his voice. "There's someone swirling around Erika and Marcus. I don't know if it's Overholt, Ellis Hanes or someone else altogether, but whoever it is, they've shown themselves to be dangerous. I'm going to need all the help I can get. Are you in?"

He didn't need to think about his answer.

"I'm in."

ERIKA PULLED THE door to Marcus's room closed. She hadn't been sure what to tell him, so she'd kept things simple, reassuring him that Lance would figure out who had shot at them and that he was safe and loved.

But her son was smart and inquisitive. He knew something else was going on. He hadn't pressed when she'd put him off, but she knew her reprieve was only temporary. Technically, she'd been lying to him his entire life. Although he was legally Marcus Powell, that was the name on his birth certificate after all, she'd let him believe a man who didn't exist was his father. She'd let him think his father was a good man who'd been killed in an accident. She'd lied and told Marcus that his father and she were only children, and that both of their parents had already passed on. She couldn't take the chance that he'd one day wonder about grandparents or aunts and uncles and go looking. It had been what she had to do to protect her son, and she didn't regret it.

But now? What was the saying? "Three can keep a secret, if two of them are dead." Now that more than three people knew her true identity, how long could she expect it to stay a secret.

She headed for the kitchen, still thinking, considering whether the best course of action was to pull up stakes and leave Carling Lake. She trusted that Lance and Daisy wouldn't do anything to hurt her or Marcus, but...

Erika pulled up short, surprised to find James sitting calmly at her kitchen table, her bottle of Jack Daniels and a glass in front of him, and a file folder to his right. "What are you still doing here? Where are Lance, Daisy and Deputy Bridges?"

"Daisy went home and Lance and Bridges had to get back to the sheriff's department. Lance said he'd send extra patrols around for the next few days."

"You didn't answer my first question."

"I'm still here because I want to apologize. I am so sorry for not having told you the truth about why I was in town."

His apology took her by surprise and cooled some of the anger bubbling in her chest.

"And I'm hoping you'll hear me out."

Erika stood silent for a moment. She wasn't sure she wanted to hear his excuses. So he was sorry, fine. An apology was worth little at this point. Her secret was out, and she was going to have to make some tough decisions about what to do about it, and quickly.

"Please?" He flashed a smile. And she hated to admit it, but the butterflies still fluttered in her stomach. Traitors. How could she still be attracted to a man who had lied to her, betrayed her and potentially completely upended her life? She didn't have an answer for how—she just knew that she still was.

She sat in the chair on the opposite side of the table from James. He poured two fingers of whiskey into the glass and slid it across the table to her.

She wasn't a drinker. The bottle of Jack had come from Daisy, left over from a rare girls' night in. Did whiskey go bad? Oh, well, she was about to find out because if ever there was a day where she needed a drink to settle her nerves, today was that day.

She took a swig. The liquor burned its way down her throat. "Okay, so I'm listening."

"When I accepted this job, when West Security and Investigations accepted this job, we had no idea why you'd disappeared."

"Isn't it enough that I disappeared? I mean usually when a person goes out of their way not to be found, it's because they don't want to be found."

"Maybe. But it's not that unusual for someone, a family or, as in this case, an executor, to engage our services to find a loved one who has been out of touch for some time. There's nothing inherently suspicious about it, although I'll admit, once I got here and met you, I did wonder why you'd gone through the trouble of so thoroughly erasing your ties to Erika Overholt. That's not easy to do in this day and age."

She gestured for him to pour another shot of Jack. "So why didn't you back off then?"

James sighed. "Because I had a job to do. One I would have never accepted if I'd known why you'd disappeared."

"That's not much of an excuse." She knocked back the second shot and slammed the glass down on the table.

The vein over James's right temple twitched, but he didn't break eye contact with her. "Maybe not, but I'm going to do everything I can to make it right."

"I'm not sure you can. You can't put the genie back in the bottle. Even if you and Lance and Daisy swear not to tell anyone my real name, Marcus knows something is going on. I'm not sure it's fair to keep lying to him."

"Why do you have to keep lying at all? I get your fear that Roger's obsession with controlling his family would lead him to try to take Marcus from you, but he's dead. He can't hurt you now."

"Can't he? Look at everything that's happened in the last few days. Look at why you're here. He's essentially managed from his grave to send you to track me down. How do I know that whatever his plan is, whatever is in his will, isn't going to be harmful to Marcus?"

"You don't, but like you said, you aren't the same woman you were the last time you confronted the Overholts. You're the strongest woman I've ever known. And now you aren't alone. You have Lance and Daisy. And me."

Erika scoffed. "You? You're not on my side. You work for Roger's estate, which is the same as working for Roger as far as I'm concerned."

"No, I don't. Not anymore."

"What do you mean?"

"I mean, I talked to my brother, and I told him I'd failed. I can't confirm you are Erika Overholt."

"What… I don't understand. I told you my real name. You don't believe me?"

"I believe you but West was hired to find you and get proof—a passport, birth certificate, marriage license—that you are Erika Overholt. I didn't do that. We're going to refund the estate's retainer."

"How can you do that? I mean, won't it hurt your company's reputation?" Was this a trick of some sort? He'd admitted he hadn't gotten the documentary proof he needed to take back to his client. Was this all some ploy to get her to show him some hard evidence that she was in fact Erika Overholt?

James shrugged as if it didn't matter to him at all whether or not his company's reputation took a hit. "Maybe. Probably, but we'll survive."

"I don't get it. When did you decide all this?"

"I called my brother Ryan, he's the president of West Security and Investigations, while you were still in the back room talking to Marcus. I briefed him on everything that's happened here and we agreed this situation has turned into much more than a simple find-and-identify case." James reached a hand across the table, stopping just short of touching her own. "We are not... I am not going to do anything that could hurt you or Marcus. You have my word on that, Erika."

Her heart urged her to trust him, but she hadn't trusted anyone in over a decade. She wasn't sure she could do it.

"How can I know you aren't lying right now? That you haven't already told Roger's lawyers who I am and where to find me and that they aren't on their way to destroy everything I've built." Or worse, somehow take Marcus from her. Just the thought had her instincts buzzing that she should grab her son and run now.

"I know trusting me is a heavy lift but I think I've

come up with a way for us to go on the offensive and maybe figure out what's going on."

"What do you mean *the offensive*?"

"I mean if the Overholts want to know who you are, I suggest you tell them."

"What are you saying?" Erika asked.

"I think you should contact the estate's attorneys and tell them who you are," James said.

The thought sent a sliver of fear singing through Erika. She'd spent the last ten years doing everything she could to make sure the Overholts wouldn't find her and Marcus. She didn't know if she could just walk into their lawyer's office and expose herself and her son to whatever Roger had planned.

"Think about it," James continued. "If you really think the attacks over the last week are tied to Overholt, the best thing we can do is get as much information as we can. And right now that means finding out what's in that will."

"Just call them up and tell them who I am."

"Exactly. The terms of the will require the executor to read the will with all beneficiaries present at the same time and in the same place. I don't know the names of the other beneficiaries, but you were the only beneficiary that the executor couldn't locate. The lawyers are in New York and he's mentioned that the Overholt family is eager to have the will read."

Erika let out a derisive snort. "I bet. Robert, Roger's youngest son, is probably chomping at the bit to get his hand on all those billions."

"Right. So he's not likely to argue if you pushed to have the will reading sooner rather than later."

She dropped her head into her hands. There was some logic to what James was proposing. If she was right and Roger's will was somehow the catalyst for the attacks, knowing what was in the will might make it easier to find whoever was targeting her.

But that would require her to trust James. Could she do that? She wanted to. Sitting across from James at the crossroads of her old life and the life she'd built for herself and Marcus, she knew without a doubt she wanted to believe in James. To trust him.

Somehow, through everything, she was falling for him. Hard.

James grasped her hand, and, as if reading her mind, said, "You can trust me, Erika. I promise you. You can trust me."

She looked into his eyes and knew he meant every word.

"Okay. I'll make the call."

Chapter Seventeen

James was right about the executors and other beneficiaries being anxious to set up a meeting. Less than
seventy-two hours after Erika had made the call to
Jenner, Hart & Black, the attorneys handling Roger's
estate, she was minutes away from finding out exactly what was in Roger's will and what it had to do
with her and Marcus. Marcus had spent the night at
Devin's so she and James could leave Carling Lake
before dawn and make the three-hour trip to Man-
hattan. The hour had been too early and her nerves
too on edge for much conversation on the drive to
the city. For his part, James hadn't seemed to mind
the quiet time.

Erika stole a sideways glance at James now as
they cleared security in the building where Jenner,
Hart & Black had their offices. Lance had increased
the frequency of patrol on her street and she hadn't
had any problems since the shooting, but James had
stuck close anyway, even going with her for the last
two days to drop off and pick up Marcus at school.
He'd installed the new tile in the bathroom upstairs

and stripped the floor of stain in the bedroom floors, staying well past their agreed upon time working on the house. Much to her surprise, Marcus, who'd never before shown a hint of interest in home renovations, had taken to helping James out after he finished his homework. They had plans to install the vanity and toilet in the bathroom over the weekend.

James insisted that he was only around so much because he didn't want to fall behind on the renovations, but she knew his increased presence, like the sheriff's department cruiser that had been making frequent passes by her farmhouse, were meant as a deterrent to any other would-be attackers. She was no shrinking violet but between the news that the bridge collapsing, the break-in at her house and now someone taking a shot at her, she wasn't too proud to admit she appreciated the company. Or that she was scared.

A young red-haired woman in a black pinstripe power suit met Erika and James as they cleared building security. "Ms. Overholt? I'm Caroline Marx with Jenner, Heart & Black. I'll be showing you to the conference room." The woman nodded at Erika, then shot a glance at James.

"I'm Erika Overholt. This is my friend, James West. He'll be joining me," Erika said, making sure her tone left no room for objection. She didn't know what she was walking into, but she knew Roger Overholt well enough to know that it wouldn't be good. Whatever half-truths he'd told her, she knew James would likely be her only ally in that room.

Caroline simply turned and headed for the elevator bank.

They exited the elevator on the twenty-third floor and passed through the eerily quiet halls until Caroline stopped in front of a set of double doors.

"Here we are." Caroline motioned toward the doors. "Mr. Jenner is already waiting for you."

Four heads turned to watch as Erika and James entered the room.

How many lawyers does it take to read a will?

A short but distinguished-looking man stood from his chair at the head of the long mahogany conference room table. "Alexander Jenner." He thrust his hand at Erika as he approached. "Mrs. Overholt, what a pleasure to finally meet you."

She felt her lips twist into a frown. "It's Powell now." She gave the offered hand a brief shake.

Mr. Jenner blinked twice. "Yes, of course, Ms. Powell," he said, his smile insincere, before turning to introduce himself to James. "I have to tell you, Ms. Powell, your call two days ago came as a welcome surprise." Jenner gestured for Erika and James to take seats at the conference room table. "Especially since our past attempts had been so disappointing." The attorney shot a look at James, who appeared unaffected by the snide comment.

"Well, I'm here now. I presume you've authenticated the photocopy of my passport and birth certificate I sent you after our initial conversation?" Erika and James took seats opposite the cadre of lawyers.

"Yes, of course. We are quite sure you are Erika

Overholt." Mr. Jenner settled into the leather executive chair at the head of the conference room table.

When she'd made the call to the law firm two days earlier to say that she was Erika Overholt, Mr. Jenner had been anything but sure she was who she said she was. In fact, she'd have placed him firmly in the skeptical category. Luckily, she'd held on to her old identification, whether to have some link to who she'd been or because some part of her knew she'd need to prove her real identity one day, she couldn't say.

Mr. Jenner glanced at his expensive wristwatch. "We're just waiting on the other beneficiaries. They should be here—"

The phone in the middle of the table buzzed. "Mr. Overholt is on his way in."

The words conjured Roger Overholt's image in Erika's mind, even though she knew it couldn't be him walking through the doors.

Seconds later, Erika heard the conference room doors open behind her.

She took a deep breath, then swiveled the chair and watched her brother-in-law Robert stroll into the room.

Robert didn't seem to register her presence initially, which gave her time to study how he'd changed over the years. Robert's blue eyes were a shade darker than Ronald's had been, but they shared the same lithe, trim frame and wavy dark brown hair. In the ten years since she'd seen him, Robert had grown to look more like his father. She couldn't help but wonder if this was what Ronald would have looked like had he lived. He and Robert had always looked so much alike.

"Mr. Overholt," Mr. Jenner said, rising and extending his hand. "Thank you for making the time to join us on such short notice."

Robert gave Mr. Jenner's hand a cursory shake. "I just want to get this over with. It's appalling how long it's taken this firm to settle my father's estate."

Mr. Jenner cleared his throat. "Yes, well, if you'll just have a seat, we'll get started."

Robert turned toward the table, then stopped. "Erika." He studied her, and Erika got the feeling that he was almost unsure whether she was real or a figment of his imagination. Then his lips flattened into a thin white line. "What is she doing here?"

"If you'll just have a seat, Mr. Overholt—" the attorney gestured again to an empty chair on the side of the table where the other suit-clad lawyers sat "—I'll explain everything."

Robert hesitated for a moment before stalking to his seat.

Mr. Jenner settled himself in his chair once again and opened the folder on the table in front of him. "We're here to read the last will and testament of Roger Overholt." The attorney peered at the group over the top of his glasses. "While it is unusual in this day and age to have an in-person reading of the will such as this, Mr. Overholt had specified several conditions that needed to be met before we, as the executor of his estate, could legally distribute his assets. One of those conditions is a formal will reading. An additional condition was that all beneficiaries be present, in person. As all the mentioned heirs, or their legal representatives, are present, this meeting satisfies those conditions."

The other three lawyers in the room wrote hurriedly on yellow notepads as Mr. Jenner spoke.

"Can we please move this along?" Robert asked irritably. "Some of us have more important things to do than give in to a dead man's whims."

Mr. Jenner shot Robert an irritated look. "In anticipation of this meeting, we have done a valuation of the estate. As of today, Mr. Roger Overholt's estate is estimated to be worth nine hundred eighty million dollars.

Her heart thumped in her chest. Nine hundred and eighty million dollars. It was more money than she could contemplate.

She glanced at Robert and watched a broad smile slide across his face.

"To my only living son, Robert, I bequeath my house in Los Angeles." Mr. Jenner read the address and some other technical information identifying the house. "The penthouse in New York." The lawyer recited the address for this property as well and mentioned stocks in several companies Erika had never heard of. "Further, although I no longer hold a position on the board, it is my wish that my son Robert be allowed to continue as the CEO of Overholt Industries as long as the Board of Directors determines it is in the company's best interests."

Mr. Jenner's eye skittered nervously over Robert. The atmosphere in the room changed instantly, as if the air now hung heavier, weighted by what the attorney hadn't said.

Robert's eyes narrowed and he leaned forward. "Wait a minute—"

Mr. Jenner raised his hand in a stop motion. "If you'll let me finish reading, I'll answer questions when I'm done."

It didn't take a mathematician to figure out why Robert's mouth had turned down into an uncertain frown. She wasn't certain what the value of the companies Robert had been bequeathed was, but she knew that the bulk of Roger Overholt's fortune stemmed from his ownership of Overholt Industries, which had not been among the names of the companies Mr. Jenner listed.

She felt herself getting lightheaded as a suspicion about what Roger had done with the rest of his estate skittered through her brain.

Everyone in the room seemed to know instinctively that whatever Mr. Jenner was about to say, it would be momentous. The other three lawyers stared down at their legal pads, avoiding looking at any of the others in the room.

Under the table, James reached for her hand, entwining his fingers with hers. She was grateful for the warmth that flowed from him.

Had Roger figured out a way to take Marcus from her? She wouldn't put it past him to reach from the grave to wreak havoc.

"To my grandson, whom I was undeservedly denied a relationship with, but who is and always will be an Overholt, I leave the remainder of my estate, including but not limited to real and personal property, stocks, bonds, securities, mutual funds and all my interests, however found, in Overholt Industries. As he is currently underage, I leave such to him in trust, to be administered by his mother, Erika Overholt, as she should see fit, until his twenty-fifth birthday."

Her stomach lurched as if the floor had just fallen out from beneath her and, in a way, it had. The attorney continued to talk, but all she could hear was a ringing in her ears. Roger had not only known about Marcus, he'd left him with almost everything. It couldn't be true. It didn't make sense.

Robert pushed to his feet, sending his chair rolling backward into the wall of windows behind his side of the table. "What kind of scam is this? You." He pointed, his finger moving along the line of attorneys at the table and stopping at Erika. "You all must be in cahoots with that woman. If you think I'm going to let you steal my father's company, you're crazy!"

Mr. Jenner stood now and looked Robert clearly in the eye. "I resent that accusation, Mr. Overholt. Your father's will is crystal clear, signed and witnessed. I have a copy here for you." He handed copies of the will to Robert and Erika.

The words on the paper were nothing but a blur. She felt nauseous, but pushed the feeling down.

"And, of course, you may challenge the will if

you choose. I will tell you, however, your father's will includes a no-contest clause. If your lawsuit is unsuccessful, you'll lose your bequest."

Robert erupted in a litany of curses. The attorneys swarmed, trying in vain to calm him down.

James turned to her. "Are you okay?"

"I honestly don't know. I don't understand why Roger would do this. What am I supposed to do?"

"You don't have to do anything. At least not right now." He squeezed her hand. "You want to get out of here?"

Erika glanced across the room. All four attorneys were still focused on Robert, who was screaming about suing them into oblivion.

"Yes, please."

They both stood, her hand still firmly in James's, and left the room. Moments later, they were outside on the sidewalk in front of the building. The snow had picked up since they'd stepped inside and a biting wind whipped it around as if they'd stepped into a snow globe.

Somehow, she hadn't noticed the building across the street when they'd arrived at the law firm, but now, looking up at the falling snow, she saw that they stood directly across from the Empire State Building.

Was that a sign, an iconic symbol of hope, as the first thing she saw leaving a meeting that had just changed her entire life?

Erika's thoughts and emotions swirled uncontrollably. She let James steer her from the law offices and to the garage where they'd parked.

Roger Overholt had never done a nice or unselfish thing in his life, so what did his leaving Marcus this money really mean?

And would she be able to handle the fallout when it came?

Chapter Eighteen

Erika hadn't said a word since they'd left the attorney's office and James was starting to worry. Learning that her son was a multimillionaire, and that she was responsible for his fortune, was a lot to process, but it wasn't his primary concern at the moment. "Mo Money Mo Problems" wasn't just a catchy name for a song. The kind of money that had just landed in Erika and Marcus's lap also made them targets for con men, thieves, kidnappers, even worse. When word got out about the inheritance, they'd both need top-of-the-line private security. Maybe for the rest of their lives.

James shot another glance across the car at Erika. She chewed her bottom lip and stared out the front windshield. Even when worried, she was the most beautiful woman he'd ever laid eyes on.

And he was going to do whatever it took to make sure she and Marcus were as insulated as possible from all the craziness that was headed their way.

He'd need to call Lance and update him on the situation. It was unlikely the media would get wind of the boy's miraculous change in fortune this soon but it wouldn't hurt for Devin's deputy father to pick the boys up from school and stay close until he and Erika got back to Carling Lake this evening.

He'd also have to speak to Ryan and get the ball rolling on a top-of-the-line security system for her home. He didn't know if it was still possible, or if Erika would even still want to open her house as a B&B, but at the very least she'd have to institute some sort of background check system for prospective guests. West could help with that as well.

"Where are we?" Erika asked as James pulled in front of a redbrick townhouse in Harlem.

"At my place. I needed to pick up a few things, and I figured we could grab lunch before we head back to Carling Lake. There's an amazing deli on the corner that delivers."

He unlocked the front door of the converted brownstone and led Erika up the two flights of stairs to his third-floor apartment. It was a shotgun-style place with the living room/kitchen space separated from the bedroom by a pass-through bathroom.

He locked the doors, then turned to Erika. "Can I get you something? Water? It's a little early but if you need it, I have wine and the hard stuff as well."

She wasn't listening to him. Her gaze moved around the room, taking in the framed drawings covering the walls. The elevated subway tracks in Far Rockaway. Two old men playing chess on the sidewalk in Harlem. A young girl falling from a bike in Prospect Park. She walked slowly past each one, studying them as if she were gazing at masterpieces hung on the wall of the Metropolitan Museum of Art.

He probably had too many for the limited space, but each of the drawings spoke to him in a different way and he couldn't imagine not being able to look up and see any of them whenever he needed.

Erika stopped in front of a drawing of a marine carrying an injured child to safety. "These are amazing. They look like photos but they aren't, are they?"

"No, they're drawings. Hyperrealist drawings."

She turned to him. "These are yours?" Her eyes scanned over the other walls. "You drew them all?"

He nodded. "It's a kind of therapy." In more ways than one.

Erika tilted her head and looked at him as if she were seeing him for the first time. "They're amazing. You're an artist."

A blush climbed the back of his neck. Her praise sent a warm feeling flooding through his body. "I don't know about that. Look, make yourself at home. The menu for the deli should be on the kitchen counter. I'm just going to pack a few more clothes, then I'll call in our order."

He walked through the bathroom, and into his bedroom, breathing out a knot of anxiety as he did. He grabbed an overnight bag from his closet. He wanted to get a few more changes of clothes since it looked like he was going to be in Carling Lake for a little longer. He began tossing shirts inside the bag while attempting to work out just what he was feeling.

He hadn't really thought about how it would feel to have Erika see his art and know he'd drawn it. It had felt an awful lot like baring his soul.

"I take it from the circle and two stars next to it that the Reuben sandwich would be your recommendation, if I asked for one."

James turned and found Erika leaning against the doorframe from the bathroom to the kitchen. He smiled. "Definitely, you won't find a better Reuben in the city."

"Why did you get all weird when we were talking about your drawings?"

"I don't think I got weird." He grabbed a pair of pants and threw them into the bag on top of the dresser.

"Hey," Erika said, coming to stand next to him. "You are so talented. You said you were looking for the next step in your life—couldn't this be it? I think there are a lot of people who'd love to see your art, to own your art."

The owner of the gallery who'd sold his last two etchings said the same thing to him several days earlier. But selling a couple of pieces was different from trying to make a living as an artist. He wasn't sure if he could do it. He wasn't sure if he wanted to do it.

"What were you just thinking about?" Erika asked.

"I actually sold a piece recently. And the gallery has asked if I'd be interested in selling more with them. Maybe even having a small show."

"That's amazing. You should do it. Or if you want,

you could open your own gallery and sell directly to people. I'm sure many of the tourists who visit Carling Lake would love to have pictures that reminded them of the lake and mountains. And you might be able to sell some to the hotels and resorts in the area."

Only inches separated them. He vibrated with the need to reach out and touch her. "In Carling Lake?"

Erika's chocolate brown eyes heated. "Anywhere. Wherever you end up setting down roots, I mean." Her voice was little more than a whisper.

"And if I were to set down roots in Carling Lake? What could that mean for us?" He reached out and gently skimmed his fingers down her arm, her skin igniting a fire deep in his belly.

"James," Erika murmured, the desire in her eyes shooting straight to his groin.

He pulled her close, and he was sure she could feel just how much he wanted her. Dipping his head, he brought his lips within millimeters of her own. "Yes?"

"Yes." She closed the distance between them and met his lips in a demanding kiss.

He deepened the kiss, his body hardening as passion raced between them.

She fit against his body like she belonged there.

He walked her backward the four steps to the bed and eased her down onto it. For a moment, he just stared down at her—breathless, her dark eyes full of desire—and marveled that this amazing woman wanted to be with him. Then he lowered himself to the bed and ran kisses down one side of her neck, then the other. Her moan nearly undid him.

"I want you," Erika said breathlessly, plunging her hands beneath his shirt and running them up his back.

He rose just enough to shed his shirt and allow her to get rid of her top.

Erika wrapped her hands around his neck and pulled his head back down into a kiss that was anything but gentle. She brought her legs up to hug his hips, sending him nearly wild with desire. He pressed into her, running a hand up her leg, to the waistband of her suit.

A moment later, they were both free of all clothing.

For a second, James couldn't speak. He couldn't even breathe.

She was the most beautiful woman he'd ever laid eyes on.

Erika stepped closer. She took him in her hand and stroked his length. He groaned, stepping away just long enough to grab protection. Erika sat on the bed, propping herself on her elbows and watching him sheath himself with passionate hunger in her eyes.

A moment later, he joined her, covering her body with his own. Erika ran her hands over his back, her eyes locked on his as he positioned himself at her entrance. He ran his thumb over her cheek, then her lips, feeling the softness of her skin as he slid into her. Her back arched, drawing him in deeper.

He held himself there for a moment, in awe that

this amazing, wonderful woman wanted to share herself with him this way.

Erika reared up, claiming his mouth in a passionate kiss. Then he began to move and he lost the ability to think about anything other than the woman beneath him. Each moan sent a surge of excitement through him. He was dangerously close to falling over the edge.

"You feel so damn good," he whispered against the soft skin just above her breast.

He slowed his pace and caught her taut nipple in his mouth. Erika gasped in pleasure and he nearly broke again. She stroked her hands over his back and hooked her leg over his hip. Pulling him closer, urging him to sink himself deeper.

James slid his hand between their bodies and cupped her center. Erika moaned, her back arching. He moved his thumb in tiny circles, increasing the speed and pressure until she cried out with pleasure.

He held her until she slumped back against the bed, spent. Then with one swift movement, he surged up and entered her again with one hard stroke. Erika's eyes sprang open, locking onto his. He saw the barely controlled passion surging through him reflected in her gaze.

Erika wrapped her arms around his shoulders and her legs around his waist, pulling him in as closely as she could while he found the rhythm that sent them both to a place he wasn't sure they'd ever come back from.

And he wasn't sure he wanted to.

AN HOUR LATER, Erika sat beside him on his couch, looking sexily rumpled and satiated in one of his collared button-downs. He had to fight to keep his mind from wandering to what she wasn't wearing under his shirt as they dove into their sandwiches with gusto. Apparently, they'd both worked up an appetite from their midday jaunt.

He watched Erika lick dressing from her fingertips and felt desire coil in his chest.

"Why are you looking at me like that?"

His answer was a smile he knew said more than any words could.

She blushed prettily and scooted farther from him on the sofa. "We don't have time for that."

"I can be quick."

Erika laughed, a sound that was quickly becoming his favorite melody. "I don't know if you should brag about that."

He slid closer to her. "I love your lips." He dipped his head and dotted soft kisses along her throat.

She wrapped her arms around his neck and let her head fall to the side, giving him better access. "And I could stare into your eyes all day long. I think they might be one of the most beautiful things God has ever graced this world with."

His lips met hers in a soft languid kiss.

He wanted to do this every day for the rest of his life. He wanted to be with Erika every day for the rest of his life. The only thing that surprised him about the realization was how right it felt.

He could have spent all day making love to her

but they needed to talk about next steps regarding her and Marcus's safety.

James rose, chucking their lunch detritus in the garbage before returning to the sofa. "There are a few things we should discuss before we get on the road."

"Like what?" Erika eyed him with suspicion.

He took her hand. "Marcus being a long-lost Overholt is going to draw intense scrutiny the moment the media gets hold of it. And the kind of money he, and through him you, now have access to will make you targets for con men and criminals alike." He could see the wheels in her brain turning, processing what he'd said and what it meant. "You both are going to need full-time security at your home and pretty much anywhere you go for the foreseeable future."

She froze, and he felt her hand turn to ice. "That's why he did it." She shook her head slowly.

He had no idea what she was talking about. "Why who did what?"

"That's why Roger left the money to Marcus."

James rubbed her hands between his own to warm them. "Baby, I'm sorry. I don't understand what you mean?"

"Everything I did—leaving, changing my name, keeping the truth about Ronald from Marcus—I did it all so that Marcus would be a better man than his father, than all the Overholts. And from his grave, Roger Overholt just made it all for nothing. Leaving Marcus that money—" Erika looked into his eyes and the despondency he saw there nearly crushed him. "Roger just made Marcus an Overholt. And there's not a thing I can do about it."

"You could disclaim the inheritance."

"It's not just about the money. How many people at Jenner, Hart & Black know about Marcus? How long do you think it will take before someone leaks that there's a long-lost Overholt heir?"

He would have liked to argue with her, but he knew she was right. There was no way Marcus's lineage could remain secret forever. Pretty soon, Marcus would no longer be an anonymous ten-year-old trying to figure out his way through life. He'd be one of the richest children in the country.

"You saw Robert's reaction." Erika was talking out loud, but the words were more for her than him. Processing the *why* of the situation. "He'll never invite Marcus into the family fold. Roger has just re-ignited the same type of feud he fostered between Ronald and Robert. Roger may not have snatched Marcus away from me, but this was his last-ditch effort to show me he still has control over our lives."

"Let me talk to my brother. I promise, you and Marcus will have the best security out there."

"I can't… I don't want to live… I don't want Marcus living in a gilded cage. I won't do it."

"West is one of the best security and investigations firms on the East Coast. I'll have him work up a design for a system for your house and a proposal for private security—" He held up a hand when she looked like she'd refuse. "Minimal, discrete protection. I'm just asking you to look at the proposal and think about what I'm saying. This is about your and Marcus's safety, Erika."

He felt guilty the moment he said it. Even though what he said was 100 percent true, it was still manipulative.

From the pinched expression on her face, Erika realized both those things and didn't like it. But after a tense moment, she nodded.

"I'll look at the proposal." She took a step back. "I'm going to take a quick shower and get dressed, if that's okay?"

"Of course."

He waited until the bathroom door closed behind her before dialing Lance's cell number.

The sheriff picked up on the first ring, as if he'd been waiting by the phone to hear how the meeting with the estate executor had gone. James filled him in quickly. When he was done, the silence on the other end of the line stretched so long he had to check to make sure their call hadn't been dropped.

"Well, say something, Sheriff."

"This is.... I don't know what it is. Amazing. Crazy. Weird. Something out of a fairy tale."

"Add potentially dangerous to that list and I'll agree with you."

"I see what you mean," Lance said after a moment.

"I think Deputy Bridges should pick the boys up from school today and maybe keep a close eye on them until Erika and I get back."

James heard a chair squeak on the other end of the line, as if Lance had changed positions. "I'll send Deputy Bridges over to the school now. The last bell won't ring for another hour or so but it won't hurt to keep an eye out."

"Thanks. It doesn't appear that word has gotten out yet, but Robert was irate when he found out Marcus got most of the estate. Who knows what he'll do or say?"

They spoke about the increased security measures that might be needed soon for a few more minutes before James ended the call.

And immediately made another.

James listened to the water running in the bathroom as he waited for Ryan to pick up, and wondered what Erika would do if he slipped into the shower with her.

"James? Are you there? We must have a bad connection?" Ryan's voice shattered the very nice daydream he'd been building.

"Yeah, yeah. I can hear you. I don't have much time before Erika and I need to get back on the road to Carling Lake but a lot of stuff went down this morning."

He ran through a slightly more detailed version of the meeting with the attorneys.

"Sounds like a doozy of a meeting."

"That's one way to put it. I want to know everything there is to know about Robert, his wife, his kids, his best friend and his wife and kids. Anybody who is in any way associated with Robert or Overholt Industries."

"Do you know how many people work at Overholt Industries?" Ryan deadpanned.

"I don't care."

Ryan sighed. "How about we start with the Board of Directors and major executives and work our way from there?"

"Fine," James gritted out.

"Now answer me this, are you just a man obsessed with protecting a woman you have feelings for or in your professional opinion," Ryan stressed the last two words, "is Robert Overholt a real threat to Erika and Marcus?"

James thought about the question. He was plagued by the thought that he'd fall short and Erika and Marcus might be harmed, but the amount of money they were dealing with made people take extreme actions. "Both."

"I guess that's fair."

"Somebody has orchestrated at least two attacks on Erika in the last week. Robert didn't seem like he knew what was in the will but he could just be a damn good actor."

"Okay, but you said the bridge thing and the shots were directed at Erika. Hurting, or even killing Erika, wouldn't mean Robert gets the money, right?"

"No, but maybe Robert doesn't know that. Or maybe he's so upset he doesn't care. But more likely, assuming Robert is behind the attacks on Erika, he's figured that as Marcus's only blood relative, he'd get custody of Marcus, and his trust, should anything happen to Erika."

"Okay, I'll put a guy on it and get back to you ASAP."

"Thanks." The water in the shower shut off. James could hear Erika moving around in the bathroom again. "I also talked to Erika a bit about the potential threats money like that can raise."

"And?"

"She's not happy about it but she's agreed to look at plans for a home security system and private security."

"I can get a team started on that, too. We'll have to send someone out to get accurate measurements. A layout. The works."

"I know the drill. I plan to broach the subject of staying in one of the guest rooms in the B&B until we've got all this sorted out, so Erika and Marcus won't be unprotected."

"Hmm."

"What does that mean?"

"Our job is technically over. I canceled the contract and gave Overholt's executors back their retainer, like we discussed. There's no reason for you to stay in Carling Lake."

"There's a reason," James grumbled. The last thing he was in the mood for was his little brother ribbing him over a woman.

Ryan chuckled. "Oh, yeah. Care to share it with me?"

"No."

He heard Ryan's chuckle turn into full-on laughter before he punched the button on his screen to end the call.

Chapter Nineteen

The multi-head shower in James's bathroom was so luxurious it had Erika entertaining thoughts of what it would be like to step inside every day. It might even make moving to a city like New York worth it.

First, you suggest James move to Carling Lake. Now you're fantasizing about moving in with him. You've lost your mind.

Maybe she had. James's prowess in the bedroom was certainly enough to make any woman go a little crazy. But that was exactly what thinking about a future with him was. Crazy.

He was a war hero and private investigator from New York. She was a mother, part-time reporter and wannabe B&B owner who lived in Carling Lake, New York. Nothing about the two of them together made any sense and she had to remember that.

She shut off the shower and got out. Toweling off, she squared her shoulders and met her reflection in the mirror.

She didn't have any regrets about sleeping with James. She'd wanted him. Truth be told, she'd wanted him from the first moment she'd set eyes on him. Truth really be told, she wouldn't mind having him again. And again. And...

But just because she didn't regret sleeping with James, didn't mean it was a good idea for them to get any more involved with each other. Geography wasn't the only concern. She also had Marcus to think about. And their life was undoubtedly about to take a drastic turn with the addition of the Overholt billions that neither of them could properly comprehend at the moment.

But despite the rational side of her brain cataloging all the reasons she shouldn't, Erika could still feel herself in danger of falling in love with James West.

At least this time she was walking into it with eyes wide open, she thought as she got dressed. With Ronald she'd been so young and the grief of losing her mother still so fresh, she hadn't seen her relationship with Ronald for the abusive situation that it really was until it was too late.

A relationship with James, she knew, was a recipe for disaster, although in a very different way from what she'd had with Roland. He did seem to feel badly about deceiving her, which might make him feel obligated to help her out and hang around until he was sure she and Marcus were safe. But eventually he'd return to New York and his phenomenal shower and she and Marcus would—

She had no idea what she and Marcus would do. A day ago, she had their futures planned out precisely, but now? Would they have to move? She loved Carling Lake and so did Marcus. But it was a small town and she knew that money like the kind Marcus stood to inherit brought with it a host of security concerns she couldn't even begin to contemplate.

Concerns which West Security and Investigations could help her with. Which was why she was going to take a hard look at the proposal from West. She stepped out of the bathroom.

The bedroom was vacant but she could hear James moving around in the living room.

She opened the bedroom door.

James sat at the edge of the couch, typing on a laptop on the coffee table in front of him. He surged to his feet as she stepped into the room.

"Hey. Hi. Hi." He rubbed his hands against the rough denim of his jeans and cleared his throat. His obvious awkwardness helped to set the butterflies in her stomach some. "I made coffee."

He rounded the coffee table and moved into the kitchen.

"Thanks." Erika followed, sliding up next to him and taking the coffee mug he plucked from an upper cabinet.

"Are you having second thoughts about sleeping together?" His voice was rough and she wasn't sure if it was just wishful thinking on her part, but she thought she detected vulnerability.

She smiled up at him, set the cup on the counter and wrapped her arms around his waist. "Well, it would be a little bit too late if I were, but I'm not."

"Good."

She felt his body relax against hers. "But that doesn't mean I don't have a ton of questions swirling through my head. Like what are we doing? Where could this possibly lead? You live here and I live in Carling Lake. And then there's all the stuff with the Overholts. And truly this just seems to be the worst time to start a relationship with anybody. Not that I'm saying we're in a relationship."

James kept his arms wrapped around her but leaned back so he could look down at her. "How about we put a pin in all those questions and revisit them at a later time. Right now we can just enjoy the moment and being here together."

It wasn't the answer she wanted, but the sparks of desire she saw in his eyes sent her questions to the back of her mind.

Her heartbeat picked up several paces and there was a familiar longing low in her body. "Umm... enjoy the moment? I'm not sure I know how to do that." She let a seductive smile slide across her face. "I might need you to show me how."

James's grin bordered on lecherous. He cupped her bottom and hoisted her up. Her legs wrapped around his waist, the feel of his hard length pressed between them, spiking her desire further.

He pulled her into a brief but scorching kiss before starting toward the bedroom. "I think I can do that."

Their second go-round in the bedroom had left Erika feeling boneless. But the tension and anxiety that had melted from her body when she'd been in

James's bed increased as they got closer and closer to Carling Lake. The meeting with the Overholt lawyers had raised more questions than it had answered. If Roger knew about Marcus, why hadn't he reached out while he'd been alive? And why would he leave almost all of his fortune to Marcus? There had to be a catch.

James's phone rang, cutting into the silence in the car.

James punched a button on the steering wheel. "Lance, you're on speaker."

"Good to know. How are you hanging in there, Erika?"

"I haven't had a complete meltdown but I'm reserving the right to do so later," she quipped.

"Fair enough. Listen, what's you guys' ETA?" Lance said.

"We're about a half hour out. Why? Is something wrong?" James asked.

"Nothing is wrong. In fact, I finally arrested several of the people involved in that gambling ring. Susan Garraus was among them." Erika stared at Lance in open-mouthed shock. Straitlaced Susan Garraus was the last person in town Erika would have pegged getting involved in illegal gambling. "Wow, I can't say I saw that one coming."

"Yeah, me either," Lance said. "We've got her dead to rights on an illegal gambling charge, but she wants to deal. She's claiming she has information on corruption within the city government, but she'll only talk to you, Erika."

"Me? Are you sure? I'm not exactly Susan's favorite person."

"She wants you. Says she doesn't trust anyone who works for the city not to cover up the information she knows."

She felt her heartbeat speed up again, only this time it was due to the prospect of catching the Carling Lake story of the year. It was a feeling she relished. She shot a look at James. "Would you mind?"

"Why not?" James shrugged. "We're on our way."

A little over a half hour later, Erika and James sat across from Susan in the sheriff's department's interrogation room. Lance had advised Susan that she could have a lawyer present before speaking to them but Susan had waived that right, saying she just wanted to get *this* over with.

Erika was just anxious to find out what *this* was.

"Okay, Susan. Erika is here. What is it you wanted to tell her?" Lance started the conversation off.

Susan shot a disgruntled look at the sheriff. "I wanted to talk to her alone."

"That's not going to happen," James said.

Erika slid a sidelong glance at him. If you didn't look closely, he appeared relaxed, almost as if they were just four friends, who happened to be shooting the breeze in a police interrogation room. But Erika had been around him enough in the last several days to recognize the tension in his shoulders and the tiny vein in the crease where his neck and his jaw met that popped when he was angry or worried.

"What he said," Lance seconded. "My time is

valuable, Ms. Garraus, so if you've got something to say, spit it out."

Susan gave Lance another nasty look before turning to Erika. "You were right about the grant."

Erika blinked, confused. She'd pretty much gotten nowhere with that story. "How was I right?"

"We applied for it, Ellis Hanes and I. Only we never planned to use the money to renovate city hall."

"Okay." Erika felt her eyebrows rise a notch. "What did you plan to do with it?"

Susan snorted. "Isn't it kinda obvious? We planned to use it to gamble. Or rather to gamble our way out of the debts we'd run up gambling."

James slid Erika a look. "I guess you won't need my contact with the feds, after all."

"Hang on. What are you all talking about?" Lance pushed away from the wall and came to stand next to the table on Erika's other side.

Susan shot a look at Erika and gave a bitter laugh. "So you haven't brought your boyfriend up to speed, I see. Smart girl. Men ruin everything, anyway."

"Ms. Garraus?" Lance growled.

"Ellis and I applied for a grant from the federal government to help with the costs of restoring city hall. Only we didn't tell anyone else on the city council because we never planned to use the money for restoration. That damn gambling outfit had sucked both of us in." Susan hunched over in her chair, as if admitting she had a gambling problem had deflated her. "My house is in foreclosure. My creditors are garnishing my wages. Not that it matters. If

I worked until I was one hundred I wouldn't make enough to pay back what I owe the bookies." Susan looked up, and what Erika saw in her eyes was almost a plea. "That's why we needed so much money. We were both in so deep only a big win was going to mean anything."

Even though she knew what Susan had done was very wrong, Erika felt sorry for the woman sitting in front of her. "How did you and Ellis come up with this plan?"

Susan's mouth twisted into an ugly scowl. "Ellis. It was his idea. I told him no, several times. But then my debt got so large and he convinced me that as long as we worked together, no one would know." Her expression turned sad now. "And that if we just had enough money to bet big, we could both turn our luck around. Maybe even win enough to actually pay off our debts and give the three hundred thousand to the town and honor the grant."

Erika worked to keep her expression neutral. Of course, the chances that Ellis and Susan would have won big enough to pull off their scheme were slim to none, especially at an unregulated, and more than likely fixed, underground gambling establishment. But gambling was an addiction, and addicts weren't known for clearheaded planning.

"How do we know you're telling the truth about Ellis Hanes?" Lance challenged Susan. "As far as I can tell, there is no evidence, outside of your statement here, that Ellis has anything to do with gambling or this grant you've told us about."

"Lance is right, Susan. Something doesn't add up. Sam Hogan walked off my renovation job because Ellis hired him to update a wing of his hotel. If Ellis is broke, how did he hire Sam?"

Susan scoffed. "Did Sam get the money upfront? Look, believe whatever you want," Susan shot back, "but I'm telling you what I know. Ellis's hotel and B&B haven't been doing well at all these last several years. The buildings do need renovations but between that new resort down Route 283 siphoning off customers and his gambling, Ellis doesn't have two nickels to rub together."

"Maybe," Lance said, "but you've still given us nothing to support that Ellis is involved in any of the things you've told us about."

Susan locked her gaze on Erika. "I know he hired that transient—" Susan made a face "—Brian, to set fire to your B&B while you were in the hospital and then sent him back to bust up the place when the fire plan didn't work out."

"Brian Whitmer?" Erika conjured up a vague picture in her mind of the man. She'd never employed him but she knew he was one of many who picked up work in town during the height of tourist season. If Susan was telling truth, Brian had not only attempted to set fire to the B&B, he'd most likely also broken in and taken those shots at her, Marcus and James.

Damn Ellis Hanes. He could have killed Marcus. It took a moment for Erika to beat back the rage that flared in her chest. By the time she did, Susan was speaking again.

"I made a tape of me and Ellis I discussing the grant. Several, actually. Once we got the money, I didn't trust that Ellis wouldn't somehow try to pin the whole thing on me if it went south. They're at my house in my safe."

Lance's expression still telegraphed his disbelief. "James, Erika, can I talk to you out in the hall for a moment." Lance started for the door without waiting for an answer.

Susan caught Erika's hand as she and James rose to follow Lance. "I want a deal, okay? I'm not going to lie about that. But I asked that you be here because I know you aren't going to just allow them to pin everything on me and brush Ellis's part in this under the rug."

Something Ellis said when he'd confronted Erika in the park the other day jumped into her mind. "Susan, did you tell Ellis that I'd questioned you about the grant?"

Susan nodded. "Yeah, I freaked out. I was convinced you'd figured us out. I called Ellis, told him everything. He told me to keep my mouth shut and you wouldn't have anything to go on."

Erika mentally slotted the puzzle pieces into place. She had thought Ellis's harassment was centered on the potential competition her B&B posed. But she could see how her questions around the missing grant money posed just as big, if not a bigger threat, to Ellis if what Susan said was true. Her inquiries could have pushed Ellis to go to extremes, like taking a shot at her outside of her house.

James waited just outside the open interrogation room door. "You okay?"

Erika looked him in the eye and answered truthfully, "I don't know."

She turned and led the way to Lance's office.

"What do you think?" Lance asked as he closed the door and took his seat behind his desk.

Erika settled into the chair across from Lance. "I believe her. I always felt she knew more about that grant than she was telling me."

"What she said makes sense," James offered.

Lance sighed. "It does, but I need more than her word to arrest Ellis. Even with the tapes, if Ellis didn't know he was being recorded, they can't be used in court."

"Lance, you have to bring Ellis in. This is about more than the grant. I think Daisy is right. I think Ellis is the person behind the attacks on me."

"Come on, Erika. Just the other day you were sure Daisy was wrong. And you have to admit there's a long way from gambling addict to attempted murderer."

"I know, but that was before we knew how desperate Ellis probably is. You heard Susan. This isn't just about rival B&Bs. Elis is facing potential fraud and embezzlement charges, in addition to the collapse of his businesses. Maybe even arson charges if you can find Brian Whitmer."

"If you believe Susan," Lance pointed out.

"The lady sounded credible to me," James said.

"Her statement about Whitmer being hired to set fire to Erika's house fits."

Erika scooted to the edge of her chair. The more she thought about it, the more convinced she became that Ellis was behind everything. "It makes sense, Lance, and who else could it be? No one else has a motive except Ellis."

"She has a point." James crossed his arms over his chest.

They fell silent.

The wheels in Lance's head were almost visibly turning. "I still don't know if I have enough to bring Ellis in. But—" Lance said, cutting off Erika's next round of arguments "—I can send a deputy to request an audience." Lance's lips twisted. "Nobody is above the law in my town but Ellis is the mayor, so I'll have to pay some deference to the office. And I'll run what we have by a judge and see if I can get a warrant to search his home and businesses."

Some of the tension in her body dissipated. "Thank you, Lance."

Lance shook his head. "Don't thank me yet. You two should go home. Nothing is going to happen tonight."

Erika followed James from the building and to his car. As much as she wanted to be around when Lance brought Ellis in, she was impatient to be with Marcus again. She'd need to tell him about his new-found wealth, but having him in her sights would ease the anxiousness she'd been feeling since finding out about the inheritance.

"You've been awfully quiet since we left the sheriff's station. Something on your mind?"

James gave her a wry look. "Everything is on my mind at the moment."

"You know what I mean. You should be… I don't know…happier. We know who's behind the attacks and I'm sure Lance will have Ellis in custody soon."

"Do we know that, though?"

"I know Lance is probably right about not having enough evidence for the court, but he'll get it. Once Ellis knows we're on to him and that Susan has told us everything, the jig will be up. I'm sure he'll hire an army of lawyers, but there won't be any reason to come after me anymore."

"I'll relax once Ellis Hanes is in police custody. Until then, it's safest if we stay vigilant."

She couldn't argue with his logic. She'd certainly breathe a lot easier with Ellis behind bars.

Deputy Clarke Bridges and his husband, Steve, had a large bungalow about two miles from downtown Carling Lake.

James pulled the SUV to a stop at the curb in front of the house.

Deputy Bridges opened the door. Erika noticed that, even though he was in his street clothes, he wore his gun on his hip.

James must have noticed as well. "Any trouble?"

Clarke shook his head. "All quiet."

"Thanks for taking Marcus to and picking him up from school," Erika said.

"No thanks necessary, you know that. The boys

keep each other company, which makes my job easier." Clarke smiled and led them farther into the house. "They are in the basement. I hope you don't mind. I told them they could play video games after they finished their homework."

"Clarke, so much has happened today that I can't bring myself to worry about video games. I'll just have to hope this isn't the game that'll rot his brain."

Clarke chuckled. "Some days are like that." He sobered. "Lance filled me in a bit about what all is going on. Are you hanging around for a while?" he asked, directing the question to James.

James's brow arched up. "For a while."

"Good." Clarke opened the door to the basement and started down the stairs. "Guys, Marcus's mom is here."

The heavy silence that answered sent an ominous chill shuddering through Erika before she reached the last step.

All the lights were on and the video game on the gigantic television screen mounted to the wall was frozen on a fight scene. The door leading outside stood open ominously.

"Boys!" Clarke hurried to the door at the rear of the basement.

James drew his gun and dashed through the open door, disappearing into the home's backyard with Erika at his heels.

Exterior lights at either corner of the house and over the door cast shadows around the home. It took a moment for her eyes to adjust, but when they did, they fell on a prone figure in the snow-dusted grass.

Devin.

Cold hard dread landed with a thud in her chest. She scanned the yard. Footprints led from the back door to the open gate in the fence at the back of the house. She moved toward the gate, but James's hand on arm stopped her.

"We don't know who's out there and you aren't armed. I'll go. You stay here and help the other boy," James commanded before taking off toward the fence, his gun still in his hand.

Every fiber of her being wanted to argue with him. Marcus was missing. He was her son and it was her job to protect him. She'd failed. She had to find him. But James didn't give her the opportunity to argue. He bolted for the fence, disappearing into the darkness.

A groan sounded from behind her and she turned toward Devin and Clarke. Devin's eyelids fluttered but didn't open. A bump was already growing at his temple. Someone had hit him, and hard from the looks of it.

Nausea roiled in her stomach at the thought of what Marcus might be going through right now. Had he been hit as well? Or worse? She had no idea how long ago he'd been taken. Was he terrified, wondering where she was and why she hadn't come for him yet?

She stood frozen, immovable by the terror coursing through her body as Clarke drew his phone from his back pocket and barked a demand for an ambulance at the dispatcher.

James hurried back into the yard and to her side. His eyes reflected the panic she was feeling. "It's too dark. I couldn't see anyone."

Erika's breath came fast but she couldn't seem to make her feet move, but her body trembled with a primal fear.

Marcus was gone.

Chapter Twenty

Erika listened to the hum of voices in the police station. Marcus had been missing for nearly two hours now, and she'd moved from frantic to numb.

Her son had been kidnapped.

Devin had regained consciousness in the ambulance to the hospital. He'd been able to tell them he and Marcus had heard a noise outside, a sound like a wounded dog, and they'd gone out to investigate. Devin had exited first, with Marcus right behind him. He'd made it a few steps from the door when he heard Marcus groan and fall. He turned to see Marcus lying in the grass, and then something hit him in the back of the head and that's the last thing he remembered.

Lance had put the entire six-man sheriff's department on finding Marcus, and the town of Carling Lake had rallied as well. Search parties were formed and fanned out despite the darkness. Erika knew they'd have to call off the search until morning if they didn't find Marcus soon.

She shuddered at the idea of her son out there,

more than likely held against his will. She prayed that whoever had taken him didn't want to hurt him.

James's words from earlier today in his apartment ran through her head on a loop. *That much money makes you and Marcus targets.*

Was that what this was about? The Overholt millions? She'd give it all away to have her son back in her arms.

James had talked with the attorneys who had assured him they had not released the news that Marcus was heir to the Overholt fortune. And Lance had reached out to Robert and his wife had also denied saying anything to anyone.

That left Ellis.

Lance had sent a deputy to his home, office, and the hotel and B&B. No one knew where he was, and Ellis hadn't answered calls from the sheriff.

Erika had considered whether kidnapping Marcus was some sort of blackmail or revenge scheme. Leverage so that she wouldn't reveal his part in stealing the grant money. What would Ellis do if he found out it was too late? That Susan had rolled on him and it was only a matter of time before Lance had enough evidence to arrest him?

Marcus would be worthless to Ellis then.

She swallowed hard and banished the thoughts that were threatening to overwhelm her.

The entire town was searching for Marcus. Lance had even looked the other way when James called his brother and got West involved in tracking down Ellis via their own sources and methods.

"Here. Drink this."

Erika startled, surprised to find Lance standing over her, holding a steaming paper cup. "It's hot tea. James says you haven't had anything to eat for hours and you need to keep your strength up."

She took the tea, only noticing how cold she was when she wrapped her hands around the warm cup. She took a sip and cringed at the sickly sweetness from too much sugar. Probably Lance's way of making sure she didn't go into shock.

"Erika, we're doing everything we can." Lance rubbed her shoulder soothingly. "Why don't you go home and try to get some rest."

She shook her head, setting the tea on the table in front of her. "I'm not going anywhere."

"It might be best," James said, coming to stand next to Lance. "If Marcus goes to the house, it would be good to have someone waiting there."

"I called Daisy. She said she'll stay at the house, just in case."

There was no way she was leaving the station. She wanted to know the minute any news about Marcus came in. Not have it filtered through Lance or one of the other deputies who'd only tell her what they wanted her to know.

"Okay, then. Hang in there." Lance gave Erika's shoulder a squeeze before he moved to the other side of the room.

Erika felt her eyes welling with tears. This is why she'd settled in Carling Lake. Because it was a community that looked out for one another. Cared for each other.

She just hoped that if Ellis had Marcus, he'd remember that he was Carling Lake, born and bred, and tap into the community's kind spirit.

James reached out and palmed her cheek. She leaned into his hand, soaking up his warmth and strength. "I saw a cot in Lance's office. You could try and get some sleep."

"I won't be able to sleep until I know Marcus is safe." She stepped into him and wrapped her arms around his waist, tucked her head into his shoulder and let the tears fall. "I just want my son."

"I know, I know. We're doing everything we can." James cradled the back of her head, his fingers massaging the base of her neck.

His phone rang, and he moved away just enough to pull it from his pocket and glance at the screen. "It's Ryan."

He walked to the other side of the room with Lance. The two of them hunched over a laptop, but from the lack of urgency in their movements, she could tell that this wasn't the call that mattered.

The one that said Marcus had been found.

She started again when her phone buzzed. She was still wearing the suit she'd worn to the meeting with the attorneys and she must have stuck her phone into the pocket at some point.

She had a text from an unknown number. Probably spam.

But the moment she opened the message it became clear this wasn't spam.

If You Ever Want To See Your Son Again, Be In The Parking Lot Behind The Station In Two Minutes. Alone. Tell No One. Your Son's Life Depends On It.

ERIKA LOOKED THROUGH the glass wall of the conference room. There was no one in the small bullpen except the twenty-something civilian receptionist who was speaking into the landline at her desk.

This had to be some kind of cruel joke.

But what if it wasn't? Two minutes didn't give her much time for internal debates.

If it wasn't real, she'd find nothing but an empty parking lot outside.

And if it was from Marcus's kidnapper?

She headed for the door to the conference room.

"Where are you going?" James's question stopped her before she crossed the threshold.

The text had said to tell no one. She couldn't take any chances with Marcus's life.

She turned back to the room, praying her face didn't give away what she was about to do. "I think I will take advantage of that cot in Lance's office."

"Good. You should rest," Lance said, looking away from the computer screen.

James stared at her. For a moment, she thought he was going to call her out, but then the corners of his mouth curved into a smile she couldn't help but find sexy despite the situation.

"I'll come get you if there's any news."

She returned his smile and prayed he'd forgive her for the lie. That is, if there was anything to forgive her for.

She wasn't sure whether she wanted there to be someone waiting for her in the parking lot or not. Unless it was Marcus, neither option was optimal.

Erika walked past Lance's office and headed for the building's rear exit.

The door opened with a soft click, and she stepped out into the night. A dim yellow bulb hung over the door and cast all the light that was to be had in the parking lot.

Her phone buzzed again.

Rear lot.

Erika scanned the parking lot. A dark sedan was parked in the last space at the far edge of the lot, barely visible. Not a single person was in sight.

Almost to the car, a voice called out, "Drop your phone on the ground."

A figure stepped out of the shadows, but Erika had already processed the voice. An icy chill snaked up her spine. "Daisy? What are you doing? You're supposed to be at my house in case Marcus comes home."

"Whether Marcus comes home or not is up to you. Now I said drop your phone."

Erika let the phone slide out of her hand. Erika felt fear warring with fury. The whys weren't clear, but what was clear was that Daisy had something to do with Marcus's kidnapping. "Where's my son?"

Instead of answering, Daisy pushed a button on the key fob in her left hand. The trunk of the black sedan popped up.

"Get in," Daisy said.

"No."

Daisy's right hand came up. Even in the dark, Erika could tell it held a gun. "Get. In."

Erika's stomach roiled, but she didn't move. If she just kept Daisy talking long enough, James or Lance would notice she wasn't taking a nap and come looking for her.

A smile twisted Daisy's lips. "Hoping for the cavalry? I'll never tell them where Marcus is and if I don't go back…"

Daisy left the rest of the statement unsaid, but Erika heard it as clearly as if she'd shouted the words. If she didn't go back to wherever she was holding Marcus, he'd die.

Erika climbed into the trunk, and seconds later she was plunged into darkness.

JAMES WATCHED ERIKA disappear down the corridor leading to Lance's office.

"She's tough. She'll be alright," Lance said from his place in front of the laptop they were using to track the search party efforts.

James knew Erika was a strong woman, but if

anything could break her, it would be losing Marcus. What had surprised him was the tumult of feelings he experienced on hearing Marcus was missing. Somewhere along the way, he hadn't just fallen in love with Erika, he'd also come to care a great deal for Marcus. So much so that if Marcus was hurt, he'd hunt his abductor to the ends of the earth, if that's what it took, regardless of how things worked out between him and Erika.

James turned his attention back to Lance and the aerial map on the laptop's screen. Ryan had called in a favor and at first light tomorrow they'd have a chopper in the air to cover the denser areas of the forest and the harder to reach portions of the mountains. And the dusting of snow covering the forest floor didn't help.

He and Lance were identifying those areas and prioritizing the order of the flyovers based on the likelihood that Marcus might be held there. James's phone rang and Ryan's name flashed across the screen.

"Got the background checks back on Robert and his wife. No criminal record or known criminal associates per se. A couple of businessmen who engage in practices that are unethical if not illegal but that's not unexpected." James could hear the flutter of papers being shifted on the other side of the phone. "We pulled Robert's finances—don't ask how. No large or unusual outlays in the last six months. There is something weird, though. It appears that Robert's salary from Overholt Industries goes directly into a trust each month and the trustee gives him an allowance."

James thought about what Erika said about finding out her house and cars were in Roger Overholt's name. "I'm pretty sure you'll find that Robert's house is in his father's name if you look at real estate records. After her husband died, Erika found out Roger, not she and her husband, owned the house they lived in, the cars, everything. It was how Roger exuded control over the family. My guess is the financial arrangement is part of it."

"A forty-year-old man who lets his father keep him on an allowance?" Ryan scoffed. "That's... something." James couldn't argue with that assessment. "Okay, the sister was harder to look into but we are the best so I found some information on her and we'll keep digging."

James felt his forehead furrow as his brain worked to keep up with what Ryan had said. "The sister?"

"Roger Overholt had three kids—Ronald, Robert and a girl, the youngest, Evangeline."

"Right. Erika mentioned a sister. She said the sister has been estranged from the family for years before she even met her ex."

"Estranged is a good way to put it," Ryan said. "There are photos with her and the family in the press until she was about nineteen. The last public mention of her I can find is in a tabloid rag. Apparently, she ran off and married the bass player in a minor league band. Roger disowned her and she, and the band, disappeared from public life."

"But you found her because West Security and Investigations is the best, right?"

"I did. She and her husband moved to California. They moved a lot until they divorced about six years ago. No children."

"And what has she been doing over the last six years?"

"Not much. She shuffled through a variety of jobs until about a year ago."

"What happened a year ago?"

"No idea. She just sort of fell off the face of the earth. I'm working on it. You'd think with a name like Evangeline Daisy Overholt Hargrove she'd be easy to find but…"

The buzzing sound in James's head blocked out the rest of what Ryan said.

Evangeline Daisy Overholt Hargrove.

Daisy Hargrove.

Daisy was Ronald and Robert's sister.

He'd speculated that Robert might want Erika out of the way so he could claim guardianship of Marcus and control over his inheritance, but he had the wrong Overholt. His theory worked just as well for an aunt as an uncle.

"Do you have a picture of Evangeline Overholt?" James asked.

"Sure. Stand by, I'm emailing it now."

James put his phone on speaker and opened the email from Ryan that had just hit his inbox.

It only took seconds for the picture to load, but he knew in his gut what he was going to see.

Evangeline Overholt aka Daisy Hargrove.

"What is this?" Lance said, leaning in to look at the phone's screen. "Why do you have a photo of Daisy on your phone?"

"Daisy?" Ryan's voice carried over the open line.

"Evangeline Overholt has been living in Carling Lake for the past year under the name Daisy Hargrove."

Lance swore and reached for his phone. "I'll get a deputy over to her house now."

"Ry, we need to know everything there is to know about Evangeline Overholt and Daisy Hargrove. Particularly every piece of property she owns within a hundred-mile radius." James doubted Daisy or Evangeline would be at her house if she had taken Marcus, but it was as good a place to start as anywhere.

He hurried from the conference room toward Lance's office. He'd promised Erika that he'd tell her the moment there was news. And the fact that her new best friend was actually her sister-in-law qualified.

James pushed open the door but stopped short of going in. It wasn't necessary. His gaze swept over the entire office once, twice, three times with the same result.

Erika wasn't there.

Chapter Twenty-One

Bumping around in the trunk of Daisy's car left Erika with a massive headache. Still, that wasn't the reason she was relieved when the car stopped.

Marcus. Daisy must be taking her to wherever she'd hidden Marcus. She'd suffer through a lifetime of headaches to get her son back.

The car door slammed and Erika could hear footsteps crunching along gravel as Daisy approached the back of the car.

Panic rose in her throat. Daisy had a gun and could easily shoot her the moment the trunk opened.

On the drive, Erika had felt around for the release lever that every trunk was supposed to have in case someone got trapped inside. Daisy must have removed it because she'd found nothing. No release lever and nothing she could use as a weapon. She was the only thing in the trunk of Daisy's car.

Erika sent up a quick prayer that James had discovered she was not in Lance's office and somehow figured out where Daisy had taken her.

The trunk popped open.

Daisy waited a foot away, her gun trained on Erika. "Get out."

Erika pushed into a sitting position, then gingerly stood. She couldn't be sure exactly how long she'd been in Daisy's trunk, but her legs had been immobile long enough that she needed a moment to ensure they'd support her weight.

Daisy jerked her head to the right. "Move."

Erika turned to see what could generously be called a wooden shack several feet away.

Was Marcus inside? The thing looked as if it would collapse under a light breeze. Had Daisy left her son in a hut that could cave in on him at any moment?

Adrenaline pumped through Erika as she hurried toward the structure, but inside she found nothing but an old length of rope and a dirt floor.

She whirled around to face Daisy. "What is this? Where is Marcus?"

Daisy laughed. "You didn't think I'd leave him here, did you? This place is on its last legs! I couldn't treat the little prince like that, now could I?"

Erika's heart thundered in her chest. The little prince. Daisy knew about the inheritance.

"How do you know..."

A slow smile spread over the face of the woman Erika had considered a friend. "How do I know Marcus is an Overholt? Oh, honey, I've known that since the moment I set foot in this godforsaken town. Trust me, it's the only reason I moved here."

Erika's head swam now, not just from the headache, but with confusion. "I don't understand."

"I know, and even though I don't owe you an explanation, I'll explain it to you. You see, about a year ago, I went to see my father. We'd been on the outs for quite a while and, well, it's not easy out here for a divorcee with no real marketable skills." Daisy scowled. "Let's just say he was not open to a reconciliation."

"What does your father have to do with anything? Where is Marcus?" Erika asked, her eyes scanning the shack for anything she could use as a weapon. She'd keep Daisy talking for as long as she could and hopefully get out of her where she'd hidden Marcus, but she couldn't count on James figuring out where she was in time.

"My father has everything to do with everything!" Daisy flung her arms out. Erika flinched when the gun in Daisy's hand swung in her direction, but Daisy didn't seem to notice. "He always has. Always wanted to control everything and everyone around him. And most people let him, but not me." Daisy pressed her gun-free hand against her chest. "I got away from him."

Time slowed down as realization dawned on Erika. "You're Ronald's sister, Evangeline."

Daisy's smile grew wide. "I haven't gone by that name in years. You know, I worried about befriending you. I know we never formally met, but I couldn't be sure how much you knew about me from being married to Ronald. Had you seen a picture of me?

Would you recognize me? I should have known when Roger Overholt disowns you, you stay disowned." Daisy's face hardened, but Erika could still see traces of hurt in her eyes.

Daisy was Evangeline. Technically, Erika's sister-in-law and Marcus's aunt. Why hadn't she said anything in the last year?

"You knew about the will, how?" Erika asked, struggling to put all the pieces of the puzzle together.

"My father told me. When I went to him a year and a half ago, it was clear he was in his last weeks of life. It was one of the reasons I asked for forgiveness when I did. I knew he'd require some groveling, and I wanted to minimize that." Daisy spoke as if what she was saying made complete sense. "He treated me like some stranger who had just strolled in off the street, asking to move into his mansion. Worse, actually. He wanted to punish me for having walked away from him, for having refused to let him run my life like he ran my brothers'. As if it's normal for a father to control every aspect of his adult children's lives. That's when he told me about the will. Taunted me about it, actually. He was gleeful about cutting his children out of everything. And don't think for a minute he cared about Marcus. He knew inheriting that kind of money would screw up any chance of Marcus having a normal life and he was proud of himself for doing it."

Roger Overholt had been pure evil until his last moments. Erika wanted to be surprised, but she wasn't. Roger had always been the kind of man who got his jollies from other people's pain.

"So what? Knowing Marcus was the heir, you thought you would come to Carling Lake and ingratiate yourself with us? When did you plan to tell us who you were?"

"When did you plan to tell people who *you* were?" Daisy shot back. "At first, I figured I'd get to know you and Marcus, we'd become friends who were family and then when I revealed who I really was, everyone would be thrilled." Daisy shrugged. "It's not as good as inheriting myself but I could get some money out of you and it would be better than nothing."

"Why'd your plan change?"

"Honestly, I could not take much more of living in this boring town. And the more I thought about it, the less content I was with accepting whatever you and your son decided to dole out to me for the rest of my life. That would be no different from living under my father's thumb."

"So you decided to what? Kill me? Were you behind all the attacks on me and the B&B?"

Daisy's smile sent a chill down Erika's spine. "Ugh, don't you listen? Susan told you, Ellis did all that. Except shooting at you. I still can't believe I missed. With you gone, Marcus would need a guardian and who better than his loving aunt. It could be some kind of heartwarming Hallmark story. The aunt who befriended her nephew, afraid to tell him who she was, until fate stepped in and she was forced to step up."

Daisy had completely lost the thread. There was no way her plan would work. Erika felt panic rising again. She needed to get away from Daisy and find Marcus. "Where's Marcus?"

"Don't worry. I've stashed him somewhere safe and as soon as I've dealt with you, the sheriff will get an anonymous call with his location."

Daisy raised the hand holding the gun.

THE PARKING LOT behind the sheriff's office was abuzz with activity. His stomach had fallen the moment he'd seen Lance's empty office. He'd known something was wrong. Erika wouldn't just take off without telling him. Not unless she felt she had to. Finding her cell phone had only confirmed his worst fears.

Now sheriff's deputies combed the parking lot, but so far they hadn't found anything other than Erika's cell phone.

Lance had already questioned the other deputies on duty and the clerk who worked the front desk. No one had come into the building and no one had noticed Erika leaving.

"James, I've got the video surveillance," Lance called from where he stood several yards away, conferring with one of his deputies.

James hurried over. A black-and-white video played on Lance's phone but it was clear enough for

James to see Erika exiting the building and heading toward the rear of the lot.

A figure stepped out of the shadows but their back was to the camera. They'd either been lucky or they'd known where the sheriff's office's security cameras were. What he could tell was that the person was short and slight.

"That could be Daisy," James said.

"The size is right but we can't tell much else from this video."

After several more moments, the person speaking to Erika shifted.

"Whoever it is has a gun." James's voice vibrated, equal parts fear and fury.

They watched in silence as Erika climbed into the trunk of a car. The figure got in on the driver's side without ever turning his or her face to the camera.

"I was hoping we'd catch a break and the recording would confirm or rule out Daisy."

"Maybe we did." James looked at the deputy next to Lance. "Rewind the video to right before the car turns out of the parking lot." The deputy swiped at the screen. "There. Now can you make it bigger? Zoom in on the plate."

"There's no way we're going to get a clear shot of that plate from this video. At least not without help."

"When the car turns out of the lot, the license plate is directly in the line of the camera. Even if only part of it is clear, we can run those digits against Daisy's license plate. It will at least give us some idea if we're on the right track."

"Actually, guys," the deputy chimed in, "I think this is a good picture. I can't make out the last two numbers but the rest is clear. HHJ56."

"Get inside and run that plate against Daisy Hargrove's," Lance ordered.

"I'm going to Daisy's place," James said.

"Let's wait for the plate information. It will only take minutes and could save us time if we're wrong about Daisy," Lance said before turning away and bellowing, "Sampson."

A fresh-faced young deputy jogged over. "I want you to go over to Erika Powell's place. If Daisy Hargrove is there, bring her into the station. Be careful."

"Yes, sir." The young deputy jogged up the stairs leading to the back door of the station. The door swung outward forcefully, narrowly missing hitting Sampson as he reached to open it.

"Sheriff, I got it." The first deputy skirted around Sampson and bounded down the stairs. "I got it. Daisy Hargrove's license plate number is HHJ5629. Those could be the last two numbers of the plate in the picture. And her car is a dark sedan just like the car in the photo."

"Good work," Lance said. "Call Judge Stone and get me a warrant for Daisy Hargrove's residence."

James was already moving toward the area of the parking lot where his SUV was parked.

"Hey!" Lance grabbed his arm before he could get too far. He nodded toward the police cruiser. "I've got the sirens."

James pivoted and picked up his pace. "Let's go."

They arrived at Daisy's house at the same time the search warrant came through. James was out of the car before Lance shut off the engine. The deputy Lance had sent to Erika's house had already radioed to say that there was nobody home at Erika's.

Daisy's small cottage was in an older neighborhood that looked to be well cared for. The swirling lights on top of Lance's vehicle had attracted the attention of the neighbors on either side.

Lance admonished the lookie-loos to go back into their homes as he dashed up the walkway.

They stood on opposite sides of the front door. Lance knocked and announced himself. There was no response from inside. He nodded toward James. "On my count. One, two, three."

James kicked the door in and followed Lance through the door, his firearm at the ready. If his hunch was right that it was Daisy, not Hanes's paid goon, who'd taken a shot at Erika, that meant she was armed and they had no idea what she might do if she was cornered.

It took no time at all to clear the small house.

Erika and Marcus weren't there.

He hadn't felt this much fear since he'd watched a suicide bomber detonate feet in front of him. Pure paralyzing fear.

"They aren't here." His chest constricted with each word. They had no idea where Marcus or Erika was. Or if they were even still alive.

Lance clasped a hand on his shoulder and gave

it a squeeze. "We'll find them. Just keep your head in the game."

James forced himself to take several deep breaths. Lance was right. He couldn't let himself think the worst. Erika was a fighter. She'd proven that by getting away from her controlling in-laws and she'd raised Marcus to be a fighter. They'd both be okay. They had to be. And they'd need him to focus.

He followed Lance back to the front of the house.

"Alright, boys," Lance said, meeting the two deputies that had just joined them. "We're looking for anything that could tell us where Daisy Hargrove is or where she could hold Erika and Marcus."

The four of them reentered the house and fanned out. One deputy headed for the back bedrooms while the second went through the kitchen/dining area. Lance and James moved toward what Daisy was obviously using as the master bedroom.

James began his search with the nightstand next to the bed while Lance threw open the closet doors. The nightstand held the usual clutter of books and discarded receipts on top while the drawer was a hodgepodge of miscellaneous chargers, pens, business cards and other junk that Daisy probably didn't even notice anymore. Nothing out of the ordinary and nothing that gave them any hint as to where she was holding Marcus and Erika.

"Hey, I think I've got something," Lance said, pulling a shoebox from the closet.

Lance set the box on the bed. Inside were dozens of photographs of Erika and Marcus, both alone and together. From the look of it, neither subject had any idea they were being photographed.

"This is…" Lance started.

"Creepy," James finished.

The more they dug, the more obvious it became that Daisy had been following Erika and Marcus for quite some time. James could see how much the boy had grown from the photos near the bottom of the box, which were clearly the earliest ones taken, to the photos closer to the top.

Lance held out one of the photos. "I remember this. This was taken at the Winter Festival last year. Daisy hadn't even moved to town yet."

"She was keeping a low profile or she had someone else taking these photographs for her. Either way, she knew who Erika and Marcus were before she moved to town."

"From the looks of it, she was stalking them."

That's exactly what she'd been doing. The thought was terrifying.

It appeared that Daisy had been planning whatever it was she was doing for a long time. At least a year. And there was no doubt in James's mind it had everything to do with the fortune Marcus had just inherited, although he had no idea how Daisy would have found out about Roger's will.

And it didn't matter. All that mattered right now was finding Erika and Marcus. The photos gave them some insight into Daisy's mind but not what they really needed to know.

Where was she?

"Do any of these photos show a place where Daisy might be able to hold two people without raising suspicions?"

Lance shuffled through the photos in his hand then tossed them on the bed and took another bunch from the box. "No. They're all of Erika or Marcus."

They had to be missing something.

"If they aren't here, Daisy has to have another place where she's keeping them," James said. "You know her better than I do. Does she have a hunting cabin? A boyfriend? Anyplace she would go besides here?"

Lance shook his head. "No other place. No boyfriend. At least, not that I know of."

"There's got to be someplace." James dropped the photos in his hand to the bed and headed for the door. "There's a room at the front of the house that looks like an office. Maybe there's something there."

Lance followed him into the small room, only a little bigger than the closet Lance had pulled the box of photos from. It was only big enough for a small desk and chair and a single two-drawer filing cabinet tucked into the corner.

"I'll take the desk," James said, already rounding it. "You search the filing cabinet. We might need to get into this computer." James tapped the silver laptop on the desktop.

"Unless we can find the password in here somewhere, I'd have to send that to the county forensics guys. I don't have an in-house hacker."

There was no way he was going to waste time

sending the computer off. If it came to it, he'd call Ryan, get West's technophile on it. It wouldn't be legal, but he didn't care a whit about legalities as long as Erika and Marcus were out there.

James shuffled through the papers on top of the desk, finding only utility bills for the residence. The first two drawers similarly yielded nothing of interest, but when he tried the third drawer, he found it locked.

He grabbed a letter opener from the pencil caddy and worked the flimsy lock until it gave. The drawer was nearly empty. The only things inside were a letter-size manila envelope and a file folder. He flipped the envelope upside down and a passport and several sheets of paper fell out onto the desktop.

He flipped the passport open quickly and confirmed that, at least according to the United States government, the woman who called herself Daisy Hargrove was in fact Evangeline Overholt Hargrove. He picked up the papers that had been in the envelope with the passport. It was a copy of Roger Overholt's will.

"Lance, I think I've got something," James said.

So Daisy knew about the money. That would support his theory about why she'd have taken Marcus and now Erika.

"What is it?" Lance crossed the room with purpose.

James passed the passport and will across the desk. While Lance studied the documents, James moved on to the folder.

"Okay, so we've got confirmation that Daisy is Evangeline."

James was only half listening. His focus was on the sheets of paper that had been in the folder. Printouts of isolated properties near Carling Lake that were for sale.

"Look at these." James spread the half dozen property listings out on the desk. Lance rounded the desk to view them more easily.

"Properties for sale," Lance said. "You think Daisy bought a place she didn't tell anyone about and is holding Erika and Marcus there?"

"I think it's worth checking out."

"You're right, but we have to prioritize. I need to send two deputies to each property to be safe and I don't have the manpower to search them all simultaneously."

James studied the listings carefully. Most of them were for smallish cabins within forty miles of downtown Carling Lake and off the beaten path. All but one.

"This one." James pointed at a listing of undeveloped lots.

Lance's forehead creased with doubt. "But this is basically just an empty lot. Looks like the original cabin burned down some years ago and there's only an outhouse and a storm shelter left on the property."

"Exactly," James said, growing surer this was the place they should start looking for Marcus and Erika the more he looked at the specs versus the other properties. "All the other properties have usable cabins on them, which makes sense if Daisy intended to purchase a weekend getaway. So why was she even considering this other property?"

"Maybe she was thinking about building from scratch," Lance countered.

"We don't have time to argue. We have to begin somewhere and I'm sure this is where we need to start our search."

Lance hesitated for a moment longer. "Okay, you and I can go to the lot property and this one that's not too far away. I'll send my deputies to the other four properties."

James followed Lance from the office, adrenaline coursing through his veins, his heart thundering.

Erika, I'm on my way. Hang in there a little longer.

Chapter Twenty-Two

Erika lunged for Daisy. The sound of a gunshot thundered through the small shack.

One corner of Erika's mind registered a searing hot pain burning her shoulder. But her entire focus was on the woman who had her son.

Erika plowed forward, tackling Daisy around the waist and sending them both into the side of the shack. The walls shook and for a millisecond, Erika wondered if the structure was going to fall in on them. It held, and she and Daisy tumbled to the ground, Daisy losing her grip on the gun. It slid across the dirt floor and into the dark shadows.

Rolling in the dirt, they each fought for a superior position over the other. Daisy clawed at Erika's neck, her hand falling away only after Erika slammed her palm into the other woman's nose.

The blow stunned Daisy and gave Erika a moment to scan for the gun. She didn't see it anywhere. And she had no idea if Daisy had any other weapons hidden away.

Decision made, Erika pushed to her feet and bolted through the door.

She sprang toward the cover of the nearby woods. Thorns pricked her legs through the slacks of her suit but she rushed forward as quickly and silently as she could. She kept an eye out for any other houses or cabins where Daisy might have hidden Marcus but there was nothing but overgrown foliage and darkness.

"Erika!" Daisy's scream cut through the dense woods.

She slid behind a massive tree trunk and held as still as possible. Her breath came rapidly, the sound of each inhale and exhale filling her brain so completely it was hard to make out any other sounds. Was that a footstep?

She had no idea where she was or how far she'd made it from the shack Daisy had taken her to. More importantly, she had no idea where she was headed. Running around in unfamiliar woods was a dangerous situation to be in. Not to mention the snow-covered ground and freezing temperatures. But then again a madwoman with a gun was even more dangerous.

How long had she been standing here? She hadn't heard anything else from Daisy but that didn't mean she wasn't still out there. Waiting.

She could stay here, hiding, but that might also mean she'd die here if Daisy found her.

She couldn't just stand here and wait for Daisy to find her. Peering around the tree, she saw nothing but darkness. Erika moved slowly, hoping the sounds of the nature around her covered whatever noise she might make.

"Erika," Daisy sang. "Come out, come out wherever you are!"

The voice bounced off the trees, making it impossible for Erika to tell which direction it came from. She had to move. She had to stay alive until James or Lance figured everything out and came for her. It was her only chance. And it was Marcus's only chance.

A gunshot tore through the night.

Erika's heart seized. Fear washed over her as she remembered the hot flash of pain from the graze of the bullet. She hit the ground, her arms covering her head.

Daisy had obviously found the gun. That or she had another handy. How much ammunition did she have? A question Erika feared the answer to. Daisy's plan was bonkers but she seemed to have thought it out pretty well. At least from Erika's current vantage point, crouched in the forest.

"I'm getting tired of this game, Erika."

Clinging to the hope that she'd see her son again, she started moving, hunched over, making herself as small as possible.

Brush grabbed at her clothing and left scratches on her face and hands but she kept moving.

"Okay, fine," Daisy's voice came again, but it sounded as if Erika had put some distance between them. "If you're alive, though, Marcus is of no use to me."

Erika froze, terror tearing through every fiber of her body.

"Maybe my best option now is to eliminate whatever witnesses I can and make a run for it. How much do you love your son, Erika?"

She knew it was a ploy to get her to stop running. Daisy had gone through a lot of trouble to have herself declared Marcus's guardian. Hurting him would mean she'd never see the money she'd done all this for. But it was also clear that Daisy was past the point of thinking clearly. The possibility of losing the Overholt fortune forever might just push her to do the unthinkable.

"Okay!" Erika yelled. "Okay, I'm coming out." She rose, holding her hands in the air and walked in the direction she thought Daisy's voice had come from.

"I should just shoot you right here," Daisy said once Erika faced her.

"No! You don't have to do this."

Daisy motioned with the gun for Erika to keep walking. "Move!"

Erika gave Daisy a wide berth and headed back in the direction she'd run from. At least she thought it was the same direction. She was more concerned about the fact that Daisy was behind her with a gun. There was nothing stopping Daisy from shooting her in the back and leaving her to die.

"You can have the money. It doesn't mean anything to me. If it did, I would have told Roger about Marcus years ago."

"Too bad for you it doesn't work that way."

"It can. I can sign it all over to you." She had no idea if that was true or not but she was willing to say anything at this point.

"You expect me to believe you'd just hand me hundreds of millions of dollars and not tell your boyfriends about all this. By the way, I would like to know how you got the sheriff and the hot new guy wrapped around your finger."

Erika ignored the last statement. "I'll say I took off to look for Marcus. Tell me where he is and I swear, I'll never say a word."

"I wish I could believe you. I was kind of starting to like you," Daisy said as they stepped out of the woods and into the clearing in front of the shack. Apparently, she hadn't gotten very far at all. "Back inside." Daisy poked the gun in Erika's back.

Once inside the shack, Erika turned to face Daisy. "Daisy, don't do this."

"Blah, blah, blah. You're a writer. This is repetitive."

Daisy's arm rose but the sound of a car's engine in the distance had them both jerking their attention to the door.

Taking advantage of the distraction, Erika charged, grabbing Daisy's hand that held the gun and shoving her shoulder into her stomach at the same time.

They hit the ground hard. Sharp pain radiated

through Erika's hip and down her leg but she didn't let go of the gun.

She slammed Daisy's wrist against the ground—once, twice. The third time Daisy's hand opened and the gun fell free.

Erika lunged for it, not wanting to lose sight of it this time. But before she could reach out and grab it, Daisy yanked her back by her hair. "Where do you think you're going?"

Erika fell on top of the other woman. If she couldn't reach the gun, she'd have to make sure that Daisy didn't get it, either.

Shifting her weight, Erika hooked her legs one over each side of Daisy's hips, straddling the other woman. She plowed her fist into Daisy's face, snapping her head to the side.

Daisy howled and thrust up with her palm. Blood spurted from Erika's nose and the pain had stars bursting in front of her eyes.

Daisy seized on Erika's moment of disorientation to flip their positions. Daisy wrapped her arms around Erika's throat. "You had to do this the hard way, didn't you?"

Erika grabbed at Daisy's hands, fighting to get air into her lungs. Daisy was petite, but greed, rage and adrenaline had given her a boost in strength. Prying her hands loose wasn't going to work. Erika pulled back her fist and plowed it into Daisy's gut.

Daisy doubled over, losing her grip on Erika's neck.

Erika rolled to her side, coming face-to-face

with the gun Daisy had dropped. Her lungs greedily sucked in air.

"Enough." Erika turned to find Daisy standing over her, the hammer that had been hanging on the wall clutched in her hand. "This ends now."

Without thinking, Erika reached back for the gun, bringing it up in an arc.

Daisy blinked, her eyes widening in surprise.

Then Erika pulled the trigger, and another deafening roar rocked the small shack.

THE SOUND OF a gunshot tore through the night as Lance stopped the sheriff's cruiser behind a dark sedan.

"That was a gunshot." James bolted from the car, ignoring Lance's shout to let him call for backup. The cruiser's headlights cast light onto the small wooden shack on the property. James pulled his gun from his holster as he ran toward the door to the wood shanty.

He burst through the door, assessing the scene in the space of a breath. Daisy writhed on the ground, bleeding from a wound to her right upper thigh.

Erika stood several feet away, a gun pointed down at her former friend. "Where. Is. Marcus?"

Daisy's only answer was a mewling sound.

If Erika had registered his presence, she didn't show it. Since the last thing he wanted was to startle her, he kept his voice low when he spoke. "Erika, baby, you can put the gun down now."

She blinked at him through glassy eyes.

James felt a stab of anger at the sight of her bloody

nose and the start of swelling around her left eye. He pointed his gun at the ground. In his peripheral vision, he saw Lance come through the door.

Erika turned her attention back to Daisy. "She's going to tell me where my son is." She held the gun out in front of her.

"You don't want to do this, Erika," Lance said.

Erika kept her eyes locked on Daisy. "She's going to tell me where my son is!" she yelled.

"I think he's here," James said.

Erika's head snapped in his direction. "Here?"

"On this property. Lance and I found the listing for this property at Daisy's house. It mentions a root cellar. Let Lance take care of Daisy and we can go look for Marcus."

Erika only hesitated for a moment before lowering the gun.

Lance moved in quickly, rolling Daisy onto her stomach and slapping his handcuffs around her wrists. He stepped back and used his radio to call for an ambulance.

"Where is this root cellar?" Erika asked, stepping into James's arms.

He held her tightly and relished the feeling of having her safely in his arms for a moment before answering. "I don't know exactly, but the property didn't look that big. I'm sure we can find it."

"Here," Lance said, moving over to where they stood. He unhooked the flashlight from his duty belt. "Take my Maglite. I'm not going to tell you we should wait for backup to arrive but I will say be careful."

James gave Lance a brisk nod of thanks and stepped back into the darkness. If he thought he had a chance of doing anything other than angering Erika, he'd have suggested she wait with Lance while he searched the property. They didn't know if Daisy had been working alone or what they would find if they found the root cellar.

If they were too late to save Marcus.... He wanted to protect Erika from that possibility as long as he could.

He walked in a grid pattern, Erika at his side, sweeping the flashlight over the ground in front of them. The foundation of what had likely been a cabin in the past was still on the property.

"There." Erika pointed, hurrying toward a spot about thirty paces from where they currently stood.

He could see it now, too. A wood door in the ground, a metal hook for a handle. Erika reached for the handle and pulled to no avail. She grabbed the handle with both hands and tried a second time.

"Hang on," James said, holstering his gun. He thrust the flashlight at Erika. "Hold this and stand back. We don't know who or what is down there."

He waited until Erika had moved away, then pulled on the handle.

The door was heavy but gave with little resistance, which he took as a sign that it had been opened recently.

James pulled his gun and took the flashlight from Erika. "Stay behind me."

They started down the stairs, each one creaking as they did. If there was someone down here, they knew they had company.

James panned the flashlight over the cellar, stopping when it landed on a cot in the corner. A small body lay prone on top, perfectly still. Marcus. His heart felt as if it was being squeezed in a vise. Beside him, Erika let out a wrenching sob.

Marcus's arms were behind his back, his ankles tied together and dirt-stained tear tracks ran from beneath the blindfold he wore, but he looked to be physically unharmed.

"Hello?" Marcus said, his voice small and hoarse from crying.

"Marcus!" Erika ran across the cellar.

"Mom!"

The sound of the boy's anguished cry for his mother tore James's heart in two. Marcus looked to be unharmed but the emotional scars from the situation could take time to show. And even more time to heal. For Marcus and for Erika.

There was bound to be a long road ahead for both of them. In that moment, James knew that he wanted to be there and travel that road with them. For the rest of his life.

Erika threw her arms around her son, holding him as they both wept with relief. James freed Marcus's hands and legs from the ropes that had been used to bind them.

Erika eased the blindfold from her son's eyes.

The flashlight gave off the only light in the space, and Marcus blinked against the sudden change.

Marcus threw his arms around his mother, and Erika drew him in, dotting his face with kisses.

James caught her eye over Marcus's shoulder. She smiled and reached out to him.

He took her hand and let her draw him into the hug. He wrapped his arms around the woman and child he'd lay down his life for and thanked the heavens they were safe.

Chapter Twenty-Three

"Okay, let's clean up these breakfast dishes and get to work on that science project," Erika said, carrying her plate and empty coffee mug to the kitchen sink.

"But, Mom, it's Saturday," Marcus whined.

"Exactly, which means you only have two days until it's Monday and the project is due. So let's get it done."

Marcus took his dirty plate to the sink, grumbling under his breath about the unfairness, before heading to his room to get to work.

She ignored him and began rinsing their dishes before stacking them in the dishwasher. The bullet that grazed her arm would leave a scar but nothing more damaging.

Marcus however had suffered through nightmares for the first several nights after the kidnapping. She'd made him an appointment with a local therapist and that seemed to have helped. He'd taken the news about his father and long-lost relatives surprisingly well. He'd taken the news about suddenly becoming a billionaire even better, starting a draft Christmas list, although it was only February. They'd already had one long talk about their newfound wealth and the importance of principles, values and character, and she could see several more similar talks in her future. But Marcus was a good kid. She had faith the money wouldn't corrupt him.

Keeping Marcus's existence out of the public eye had been impossible after Daisy's arrest. James's brothers Ryan and Sean had rolled into Carling Lake the day after they'd found Marcus with several other men and enough equipment that you'd have been forgiven for thinking they were about to launch a shuttle into space. Installing the security system took three days, but she had to admit she'd never felt safer. Especially since they'd also left bodyguard Tess Stenning behind.

Although she had vowed to be far more careful about who she befriended in the wake of Daisy's betrayal, she'd found Tess to be a consummate professional with a quick wit that was disarming.

Tess was the first paying guest at the B&B, but she hadn't been the only paying guest. Tess had shown up in Carling Lake, along with Brandon West, James's lawyer brother. Brandon had been a godsend, explaining what to expect while Roger's will was working its way through the system and putting her in touch with a financial planner and accountant with experience in handling the amount of money Marcus was about to come into. Guess you couldn't just walk into Bank of America and open a billion-dollar checking account.

She'd also had Brandon reach out to Robert through his lawyers. She would never forget what Roger and Ronald had put her through but maybe this could be an opportunity for the family that was left to start anew. Without Roger's menacing presence lurking over the Overholts, maybe they could build some semblance of a functional relationship. So far she'd heard nothing from him, though. Not about fighting the will or getting to know Marcus.

For the hundredth time, she glanced out the window over at the now-empty structure next door. Technically, James still had a few days left on his lease, but the cabin had been vacant for the last two weeks and three days, ever since he'd headed back to New York.

They'd spoken every night since he'd left, but conversations had become more and more strained. With each passing day, the question that neither of them seemed to want to tackle grew bigger and bigger. Where was their relationship headed?

In those moments in the back of Daisy's car, the answer to that question had crystallized for Erika. She wanted to be with James.

But pride and fear had kept her from telling him as much before he'd left for New York, even though part of her suspected he felt the same way. Thankfully, she'd only been grazed by the bullet to her arm and hadn't required a stay in the hospital. James had stuck around long enough to make certain she was okay and to finish the renovations on her house but then he had to go back to New York, giving her no sign about when, or if, he planned to return. The last two weeks hadn't been a complete downer, however. Brian Whitmer had been arrested by authorities in Ohio during a traffic stop. It hadn't taken much convincing to get him to confess. Ellis had hired him to set a small fire at the B&B to bolster Ellis's claims that it was unsafe for visitors. When James thwarted the arson attempt, Brian had returned, intending to cause enough damage to keep the B&B from opening on time.

Ellis had come to him again, desperate and nearly crazed. He'd decided that if Erika opened her B&B, then that would be the final straw for his family's hospitality company. Never mind that the debt he'd amassed stealing money from the company to support his gambling habit. But desperate people weren't always the most rational. Brian had cut a deal to testify against Ellis and a few days after his arrest, Canadian Border Services stopped Ellis trying to cross into Ontario using a fake ID.

Of course, Ellis denied any involvement and claimed the fraudulent grant was all Susan's idea, but Lance seemed confident that there was enough to put Ellis away for several years. Ellis's sister had stepped up to manage the B&B and hotel but no one knew for sure what was going to happen to the family's businesses.

Unlike Ellis, Daisy appeared to be eager to take a plea. She'd been arrested and charged with two counts of kidnapping, the assault on Devin and a host of other charges. Robert had put out a statement disavowing Daisy's actions and stressing that she hadn't been a part of the Overholt family for many years. With multiple attempted-murder and kidnapping charges, among the many other charges she was facing, throwing herself on the mercy of the court was the only way she was ever going to see the light of day again. She was looking at decades in prison and Erika hoped she ended up serving every minute. As far as she was concerned, it was the only way to ensure Marcus's safety.

Her phone rang as she started the dishwasher. The main number for the *Carling Lake Weekly* scrolled across the screen.

"Erika, it's Aaron." Her boss's voice boomed through the speaker. "I know it's the weekend, but I just had a story come across my desk that I want you to get a jump on."

She'd already given Aaron her notice but had agreed to stay on until he could hire someone to fill her position.

"What is it?"

"I think it would be better if I explained it to you in person. Can you come into the office now?"

"I have to find someone to stay with Marcus."

"Bring him. He can sit at Margaret's desk and play on the computer."

"We'll be there in fifteen minutes."

She disconnected the call and hurried an excited Marcus into the car.

It wasn't often that Aaron got a hot tip on a story. Actually, in the eight years she'd been working for the *Weekly* this was the first time she could remember it ever happening.

The *Weekly*'s lobby was pitch-black as she pulled open the doors. She grabbed hold of Marcus's hand as they stepped into the dark space.

"Hello? Aaron? Are you here?"

The overhead lights rose slowly. The framed *Weekly* covers that had graced the lobby walls since she'd started working for the paper were gone, replaced with drawings Erika immediately recognized as James's work. Multiple pieces hung on the wall. Some of them she recognized from his apartment, but others were unfamiliar.

A black-and-white drawing in pen depicting the *Weekly* building. A rendering in color of Carling Lake and the surrounding mountains.

An easel stood in the middle of the space. On it was a canvas-sized drawing of her and Marcus laughing, their arms wrapped around each other.

"Cool," Marcus said in an almost reverent whisper.

"While I was in New York..." A familiar deep voice came from above their heads.

Erika pulled her gaze away from the drawing and watched as James descended the stairs leading from the upper offices, wearing a dark suit and white dress shirt.

"...desperate to be back here with you and Marcus, I'd close my eyes, and that's how I envisioned you two."

"You were desperate to get back to us?"

James came to a stop, feet from her. "Honey, you have no idea. I wasn't back in New York for ten minutes before I realized my home was with you and Marcus."

"But when we spoke on the phone... I wasn't sure..."

James took her hands in his. "I wanted to give my brother two weeks' notice, and I needed to sublet my apartment. And I wanted to finish this. A grand gesture of sorts. I've decided to take your advice. Aaron has agreed to rent the *Weekly*'s lobby to me to use as a gallery here in Carling Lake. I'll also have a few pieces with a gallery in New York and the owner is going to help me get the word out about this place."

Erika's heart thundered with excitement. "So you're moving here, to Carling Lake, permanently?"

"If you'll have me?" James gave a tentative smile, his gaze moving from her to Marcus and back.

Erika looked at Marcus. "What do you say?"

"Yes! Yes! Yes!" Marcus beamed.

Erika wrapped her arms around James's neck, pulled him close, and smiled. "I guess it's unanimous, then."

"I love you, Erika Powell."

"And I love you, James West."

* * * * *

H HARLEQUIN
INTRIGUE

#2091 MISSING WITNESS AT WHISKEY GULCH
The Outriders Series • by Elle James

Shattering loss taught former Delta Force operative Becker Jackson to play things safe. Still, he can't turn down Olivia Swann's desperate plea to find her abducted sister—nor resist their instant heat. But with two mob families targeting them, can they save an innocent witness—and their own lives—in time?

#2092 LOOKS THAT KILL
A Procedural Crime Story • by Amanda Stevens

Private investigator Natalie Bolt has secrets—and not just about the attempted murder she witnessed. But revealing her true identity to prosecutor Max Winter could cost her information she desperately needs. Max has no idea their investigation will lead to Natalie herself. Or that the criminals are still targeting the woman he's falling for...

#2093 LONE WOLF BOUNTY HUNTER
STEALTH: Shadow Team • by Danica Winters

Though he prefers working solo, bondsman Trent Lockwood teams up with STEALTH attorney Kendra Spade to hunt down a criminal determined to ruin both their families. The former cowboy and the take-charge New Yorker may share a common enemy, but the stakes are too high to let their attraction get in the way...

#2094 THE BIG ISLAND KILLER
Hawaii CI • by R. Barri Flowers

Detective Logan Ryder is running out of time to stop a serial killer from claiming a fourth woman on Hawaii's Big Island. Grief counselor Elena Kekona puts her life on the line to help when she discovers she resembles the victims. But Elena's secrets could result in a devastating endgame that both might not survive...

#2095 GUNSMOKE IN THE GRASSLAND
Kings of Coyote Creek • by Carla Cassidy

Deputy Jacob Black has his first assignment: solve the murder of Big John King. Ashley King is surprised to learn her childhood crush is working to find her father's killer. But when Ashley narrowly fends off a brutal attack, Jacob's new mission is to keep her safe—and find the killer at any cost.

#2096 COLD CASE SUSPECT
by Kayla Perrin

After fleeing Sheridan Falls to escape her past, Shayla Phillips is back in town to join forces with Tavis Saunders—whose cousin was a victim of a past crime. The former cop won't rest until he solves the case. But can they uncover the truth before more lives are lost?

HICNM0722

Don't miss the next book in

B.J. DANIELS

Buckhorn, Montana series

Order your copy today!

HQNBooks.com

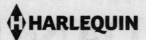

HARLEQUIN

Heartfelt or thrilling, passionate or uplifting—Harlequin is more than just happily-ever-after.

With twelve different series to choose from and new books available every month, you are sure to find stories that will move you, uplift you, inspire and delight you.

SIGN UP FOR THE HARLEQUIN NEWSLETTER

Be the first to hear about great new reads and exciting offers!

Harlequin.com/newsletters

The Big Island Killer is terrorizing the women of Hawaii and it's up to Detective Logan Ryder and his task force to find and capture this elusive criminal. Then he meets and falls for Elena Kekona, who matches the victims' profile, and suddenly the case becomes very personal...

Keep reading for a sneak peek at
The Big Island Killer,
the first book in R. Barri Flowers's Hawaii CI series.

"How did you end up on the Big Island?"

"To make a long story short, I was recruited by the Hawaii Police Department to fill an opening, after working with the California Department of Justice's Human Trafficking and Sexual Predator Apprehension Team. Guess I had become burned out at that point in investigating trafficking cases, often involving the sexual exploitation of women and children, and decided I needed to move in a different direction."

Elena took another sip of her drink. "Any regrets?"

Reading her mind, Logan supposed she wondered if going after human traffickers and sexual predators in favor of serial killers and other homicide-related offenders was much of a trade-off. He saw both as equally heinous in nature, but the incidence was much greater with the former than the latter. Rather than delve too deeply into those dynamics, instead he told her earnestly, while appreciating the view across the table, "From where I'm sitting at this moment, I'd have to say no regrets whatsoever."

She blushed and uttered, "You're smooth in skillfully dodging the question, I'll give you that."

He grinned, enjoying this easygoing communication between them. Where else could it lead? "On balance, having the opportunity to live and work in Hawaii, even if it's less than utopia, I'd gladly do it over again."

"I'm glad you made that choice, Logan," Elena said sincerely, meeting his eyes.

"So am I." In that moment, it seemed like an ideal time to kiss her—those soft lips that seemed ever inviting. Leaning his face toward her, Logan watched for a reaction that told him they weren't on the same wavelength. Seeing no indication otherwise, he went in for the kiss. It was everything he expected—sweet, sensual and intoxicating. Only when his cell phone chimed did he grudgingly pull away. He removed the phone from his pocket, glanced at the caller ID and told Elena, "I need to get this."

"Please do," she said understandingly.

Before he even put the phone to his ear, Logan sensed that he would not like what he heard. He listened anyway as Ivy spoke in a near frantic tone. Afterward, he hung up and looked gloomily at Elena, and said, "The body of a young woman has been found." He paused, almost hating to say this, considering the concerns he still had for the safety of the grief counselor and not wanting to unnerve her. But there was no denying the truth or sparing her what she needed to hear. "It appears that the Big Island Killer has struck again."

HIEXP0722

Love Harlequin romance?

DISCOVER.

Be the first to find out about promotions,
news and exclusive content!

Facebook.com/HarlequinBooks

Twitter.com/HarlequinBooks

Instagram.com/HarlequinBooks

Pinterest.com/HarlequinBooks

YouTube.com/HarlequinBooks

ReaderService.com

EXPLORE.

Sign up for the Harlequin e-newsletter and
download a free book from any series at
TryHarlequin.com

CONNECT.

Join our Harlequin community to
share your thoughts and connect
with other romance readers!
Facebook.com/groups/HarlequinConnection